a
♡ tia ♡
tale

The Skinny Girl's Guide: to Channeling the Fat Girl Inside

A REIGNSTORM PUBLISHING

MINNEAPOLIS MINNESOTA

PUBLISHED BY REIGNSTORM PUBLISHING
Minneapolis, Minnesota

Copyright © 2015 by Shawn Michelle Johnson
ISBN: 0-9721246-8-3

Printed in the United States of America

Book design by Miki Starr for Starr Eclectic Concepts

Cover illustration by Ronnie Boykin Jr

Illustration colorization by Derwin Alexander

www.mikistarr.com

*"I know enough to know I'm not yet where I'm going to be...
I'm always becoming."*

~Ruby Dee

For Kyla Simone and Erika.

AJ's Weight-Gain Journal:
~~10~~ 6 tips to gain weight

1. eat more often

2. candy, chips, & soda

3. the "eat then sleep" technique

4. lots of water (I think)

5. big meals

6. fried foods

7. ~~no sports~~

8. ?

9. ?

10. ?

Ali AJ

My name is Alijah.

I'd prefer to be called AJ but for some reason everyone insists on calling me Ali. And not *Ahh-lee* like Mohammed, the old school boxer from like back in the forties or fifties, or whatev. And not *Al-I* because that just really sounds dumb, though it actually makes more sense. No, the correct pronunciation is Al-EE like the place where businesses throw their leftover food at night or where people leave their old furniture when they move or just don't want it anymore. Alley. SMH.

Mom says it was Daddy's idea to call me Ali so that's why I don't fight against it too much. Daddy, for whatever reason, thought it was a good idea. He's dead now so I can't really confront him about his foolish decision in applying a nickname that would forever be my label whether I like it or not. But for some reason I really don't

1

think my dad would toss or turn in any way if the rest of the world got with it and just called me something sensible. Like AJ. Besides, it was his name for me and therefore should be sacred, should it not? But that won't happen because people are too stubborn to support my desire for change. And so, Ali it is.

Sigh...I still get sad at times when I think of Daddy. I don't cry though. Not since I was 8. My dad, Carl McKenna, died when I was just 7. He was a cop and got shot while off duty. Yeah, you heard that right – off duty. Some stupid boy was trying to beat up his girlfriend and my dad, forever the hero, intervened. The even stupider girl [and yes, I know stupider is not a word and my highly educated mother would kill me for using it] got angry that my dad was hurting her guy. She ran to their car and grabbed the guy's gun and shot it. She said she wasn't trying to shoot him, just scare him off.

But just like that, Daddy was gone.

It was real hard after 'cause my mom just couldn't stop crying long enough to do anything useful and my aunts, my mother's sisters [and there are like 6 of them], stepped in to care for me and my siblings. I don't know how anyone found time to cry in that house with all the people here and there. Every time I blinked, sneezed, coughed, or peed one of my aunts was there to oversee it on my mother's behalf.

Millie took it nearly as hard as mom and he wasn't even her real dad. Millicent is my older sister and the unfortunate product of an affair my mother had, prior to meeting D'asia's and my father, with a Cuban/Dominican American that she met while backpacking through Europe. If I didn't think that God would possibly deny me passage into heaven, I would hate Millie but I'll explain that a little later.

D'asia is my younger sister; I'm barely a year older. Though she's the smartest of us all, she just could not seem to grasp the reality that our dad would not be returning to us. Every night for a month – and I do mean every single night – D'asia would crawl in bed beside me and ask, "Ali, is Daddy coming home tonight?" And every night I had the unfortunate duty to respond, "No, D'asia. Daddy lives with God now. He's not coming back."

For the first year I didn't shed one tear. I was angry with Daddy for leaving so abruptly and making Mom and Millie sad and causing my aunts to take over our home. Besides, even if I had it in me to cry I certainly could not. While my aunts took turns tending to the elder women of my home [let us pause here and see if I can successfully name them all in order by age: Veeona, Yashika, Jadonna & Jaclyn the twins, Renee, mom fits in here, and Corecia who actually now lives in Decatur, GA], I was left to mother the aloof D'asia.

My lack of waterworks seemed to give the impression that I was okay and didn't need anyone to look after me emotionally. So I didn't [got that?]. At least not until late the following year when mom met, fell in love with, and accepted a marriage proposal from Laurence Carter. I ran away every chance I got, if you count showing up on my best friend Justin or my other bestee Erika's front porch running away. Wasn't too hard for anyone to find me and drag me by the ear and fuming back home.

So that's the legacy that my daddy left me. A nickname that on paper looks like the name of his fav boxer. OMG! I can't believe it just hit me now while I'm talking to you. That's why he called me Ali. Eh, well I guess the name isn't so bad but feel free to call me AJ if the mood strikes.

Big & Small Differences

Clearly I come from a huge, estrogen filled family. That is another source of contention in my life. Contention: A struggling together in opposition; strife. I learned that word today. Mom keeps a calendar posted in the kitchen and insists that we all learn the Word of the Day and use it in a sentence as often as possible to cement it into our brains. Unlike D'asia, I'm only good for the day I learn the word. There's just one slot available for new vocabulary; tomorrow it will certainly be replaced with the next word. Guess in that sense I'm way better than Millie who forgets the word the moment she walks out the door.

Growing up in a family made up mostly of super strong and dominant women is one thing. I can pretty much handle that. I am so totally a descendant of the Greene clan [my mom's maiden name] in that respect. Unfortunately for me, that's where similarity draws a crazy line.

Okay, so for this to make any sense, I'm going to have to paint you a mental picture of myself. My skin is sort of a mix between copper and fallow [I learned to recognize the color in Mrs. Borstein's art class. You might wanna Google it]. My eyes are a deep brown and sorta almond shaped. People tell me that I have a great smile and since Mom is such a stickler for dentistry, none of us have any issues with our teeth. Most definitely oral hygiene is on point which is the key to making a great first impression.

My seal brown hair [yet another color learned courtesy of Borstein] is pretty long, hangs just beyond my shoulders and naturally curls. I keep it in a ponytail or two braids most of the time since:

a.) I don't know what else to do with it and…

b.) I play sports and it would get in my way.

None of that is very significant.

But this is and this is the detail about me that you mustn't forget: I am 4 feet and ¼ inch tall and weigh in at exactly 98 lbs.

Now, in order for you to get why this stat is sooo disturbing you must first understand what sort of physical attributes the women in my family possess. Of all the Greene women living in various sections of Eden Grove, my mother is the smallest of them all, standing at 5'4 ¾" in height and weighing in at a hearty 165 lbs [and she would kill me if she knew I was telling you this]. Their heights range from mom's to Aunts Jaclyn and Jadonna who are both 5'7 and weight gets as high as the 265 lbs that make up Aunt Veeona.

Now I wouldn't call them fat [I would NEVER call them fat. I value my life too much]. According to Aunt Vee the women in my family are robust. So sure there are like a gang of adjectives you could use here:

Thick

Big-boned

Brickhouse

Chunky

Fluffy

But Aunt Vee [and the crew agrees] those terms are rude, crass and furthermore don't do them justice. And the term Diva is just plain overused in her infinite wisdom. So my aunts and my mother consider themselves as: Robust Beauties.

And although their sizes vary and some are more robust than others, most all of the women in my family share a common thread when it comes to things like height and curves. Even Millie, who has managed to maintain her size 4 frame throughout her entire high school career, is lucky enough to be 5'6" with D-cup boobies.

With nearly every woman around me leading with their breasts makes life a little challenging considering I pretty much have... well...none. An A cup. That's all. I suppose an A isn't the worst since Wikipedia says the smallest is a double A. But if that isn't bad enough, my family doesn't let me forget that I have the breast size of an overweight teenage boy! Ugh!

I get so sick of hearing about how awesome it is to be a woman with curves and how sorry they are for poor l'il me:

"All these skinny little white gals and black gals out here trying to get that silly-cone mess stuffed under they skin to get what God done blessed the Greene girls with! Well...almost all the Greene girls." That's Aunt Yashika [who we call Tee Tee Yashi].

"You gone be alright, Ali-girl. When you get some babies I bet all that gone just fill right in!" That would be Aunt Vee, despite the insensitive comment, the best auntie in all the world.

They are so over it [as in the hill for you other fogies, if you're nosey enough to be reading this] and I am so over them.

And Erika and Simone aren't helpful – at all. They're my BFF's but sometimes they are so completely insufferable. Simone developed first. Got her period a couple summers ago and was borrowing her mom's good bras by 7th grade. Erika's puberty gene didn't kick in too far behind. And even though Reilly [Simone's and my friend. Erika and Reilly can't stand each other] is as prepubescent as me up top, her rump more than makes up for her lacking in the upper region. Not to sound racist but who knew a regular ol' Caucasian girl could have it going on like that? Woe is me.

 Sibling Rivals

Despite my envy over their expedited development, if it wasn't for Erika and Simone, I would not have sisters.

I get it. To you this makes no sense. What about this Millie and D'asia that I have spoken of over the past six pages? Sure, courtesy of a biological connection to one Sha'Toya Bernadette Greene-Carter [who goes by Dette and will always be Greene-McKenna to me], the three of us indeed *are* siblings. Even better, sisters. But only biology dictates that. And biology couldn't have gotten it any more wrong.

Exhibit A Millicent Ezan Torres-McKenna

So, like I said before, Mom went all Woodstock back in the day and took a hiatus from her dorm at Bethune-Cookman College after her third year. Instead of going home for summer break as she normally would and as my grandparents expected, she channeled her inner renegade and took all the money she'd saved from doing odd jobs over the prior year and boarded a plane for Europe.

She was gone for a month and a half and apparently my grandmother Ophelia nearly went out of her mind from worry and rage. She saw Paris, London, and Amsterdam, just to name a few. It was in Venice that she met Yoan Oliva-Torres, a budding entrepreneur [now super successful and super-super wealthy] and fell in young-love. They spent the rest of her time there together doing goodness knows because when she came home to face my grammy and grandpa, she was carrying the spawn of Satan in her womb.

Millie, in a word is…well…Mom would so totally kill me if I

say the word that she is. So let's just say it starts with the second letter of the alphabet and rhymes with the first syllable of kitchen. And she hates me. She doesn't like D'asia either but I think she kinda has a soft spot for her that she hates to 'fess to. She has no soft spot for me. And yea, it's pretty sad but no woe-is-me just 'cause my stupid older sister thinks I'm a pain. I think she's a spaz and a complete and utter lame and so we have something in common.

Now let's see if you're paying attention. Mr. Torres is rich. Fabulously so. He, like, invented some fantastic tactic for doing investment banking [who knows, I don't ask questions. I just know he's a rich man that makes richer men even richer]. Mom is pretty open about her past but she stops shy of spilling the real about what happened after she told Yoan she was carrying his kid. The memory kinda sets her off.

So here's the cliff notes version as I've pieced together. Mr. Torres was still kinda struggling at the time but he came and swept my mother off her feet and vowed to take care of her and his kid forever. Then he caught the big fish, got really rich really fast, traded in his Volvo for a Beemer and mom in for the dark haired, olive skinned, accented, imported beauty Frederica who is now his wife and mother of the sons he's always wanted.

Fine by me cause it made Mom available to be with Daddy and have D'asia and me. But for Millie, for as much as she loved my dad and he loved her, this was really the beginning of her nightmarish existence. Here's the dealio: Mr. Torres was so happy when Frederica had their first kid Gabe, that he hardly spent any time with Millie at all. And two years later when Millie was 7 and Jorge was born, he was out of her life altogether in the physical sense.

You think I should feel sorry for her, don't you? Yea, it sucks he's not there for her. But as a consolation he gives her anything she wants. And I do mean – anything. For her 10th birthday she wanted this Tiffany charm bracelet and to have her birthday party with ten of her closest friends at Magic Kingdom. Not only did she get the bracelet, she got earrings to match. And when Mom insisted that D'asia and I get to go with to her party, Millie had such a fit that Mom canceled it and made her have a party at the local Chuck E Cheese and invite her entire 5th grade class. She fumed the entire time.

That was the first of many occasions that Mom's authority trumped that of Mr. Torres. She didn't think it fair that Millie got whatever she asked for when me and D'asia could not. And well… Mom's right. It is sorta sucky when there's so much we want and can't have. But still, it's not like it's our doing. We never complained about it. Still…Millie blames us and it shows.

Exhibit B: D'asia Raquel McKenna

Sister #2 is a different breed altogether and like Millie, I think I hold a soft spot for her as well. With that said, it's misleading to say that I like her. Not completely. D'asia's been different since she was little. We're just a year apart so we should be like, total BFF's. Not. We couldn't be anymore different. While I was throwing my alphabet soup on the kitchen floor, D'asia was spelling words with hers. When I was splashing in mud puddles on rainy days, D'asia was conducting archeological digs and trying to prove that Native Americans used to set up shop on our property.

She's a total recluse who rarely sees sunshine because she's always shut away in her room with her nose stuck so far in a book that often we forget she's even here. She doesn't care enough to comb her hair so I've taken up the habit of carrying a comb and brush at all times just to make her look presentable on the bus before we arrive at school. I don't know what she'll do next year when I'm gone. She frequently doesn't quite match and mom's eyeglass frame choice doesn't help much. Woe is Dull D'asia.

Surprisingly no one really bothers her. I think it's because Millie was like, the queen of Arthur Ashe and she probably put out an order of protection on poor little D'asia. And though she wants to hate her as much as she hates me 'cause mom puts limits on her materialism, I think part of her feels sorry for D'asia. Like, she thinks something is mentally wrong with her. But nothing is wrong with D'asia. She's just socially underdeveloped. Most geniuses are and I am convinced, even if no one else is, that my little sister is some sort of genius.

Okay, so what's the prob? Not her smarts. I'm proud of that. But…well, because she's so smart, I always have to take a back seat. Millie can have what she wants mostly. All she has to do is send her dad a memo. In a sense, D'asia is just as privileged. I love sports. Love 'em. Looooove 'em. All of 'em. But with Mom, academia always trumps athleticism. Always. Period. No questions asked. I need money for a new uniform for soccer and D'asia needs money for space camp, who do you think is getting a check and who is going on a fund-raising quest, scouring the neighborhood for odd jobs?

Now I think you're getting it. Siblings.

The only one that doesn't give much grief is my little brother Maddex. He's only 3 and the product of Mom's union with her husband of four years, Laurence. I used to run away when Mom and Laurence were first planning to get married but he's grown on me since. I guess he's not such a bad guy. He loves us and treats us as his own and he's an awesome dad to little Maddie.

Maddex has been a joy since he was born and he seems to be all that me and my stupid sisters have in common. He's what keeps us kinda bonded. I just hope he doesn't become a nuisance like them when he gets older.

Ali M (super fad!)

So, that's me in a nutshell. Alijah "Ali [AJ]" Dominique McKenna. I'm newly 14 and in the 8th grade and am sooo thrilled to be leaving Arthur Ashe behind. It's a cool place to go to school and I like most of the teachers [except my Aunt Renee 'cause she teaches my Language Arts class this year and insists I call her Mrs. Jackson and scolds me in front of the class when I forget and call her Auntie Nay even though everybody knows I'm her niece and she says, "There will be no special treatment, Ms. McKenna" though in my opinion she treats me especially different just 'cause we're related].

Next month is graduation and I couldn't be happier. Though Millie's been gone for three years, her legacy remains and because of it I'm always being reminded how I'm "nothing like your big sister, Millie. She's so beautiful and charismatic. Such a delight." Notice they don't say how "she is so intelligent." They save that for the comparison between me and D'asia. That's another reason I am only too thrilled to leave this school behind. I must break away from these girls and find my own identity without them.

Now of course Millie will be at Wilma Rudolph High when I get there. And I am so sure she's just as legendary there as she was in elementary school, especially since she started modeling last school year. But I'm mentally prepared for dealing with that and without D'asia there, it'll be a little easier to do so. And since Mom promised that I could go to soccer camp this summer, I'll be more than ready for varsity try-outs [who needs frosh-soph?].

Yeah, it's going to be so completely awesome. A new school. A new life with new and more advanced sports. A chance to start over and show everyone that just because I'm small doesn't mean that my presence isn't big. Finally, a chance to make my mark on the town of Eden Grove. And with Erika, Simone, Justin, and Reilly by my side, what could possibly go wrong??

Arthur Ashe

Teachers Suck 🐌

Mrs. Parker is standing in front of the blackboard lecturing about...about...well, about something. IDK what, I've turned down the volume completely. I have better things to think about besides recapping Newton's two laws of motion. Or was it three laws? Eh. What does it matter? Okay, I suppose some of the lecture seeped through my defenses. Better make 'em higher. Besides, who really cares at this point? I'm so sure I passed else she would have told Auntie Nay – I mean, Mrs. Jackson – who would have told Mom who would have already grounded me before report cards even come out.

Graduation is three weeks away and there is sooo much to do. There's the 8th grade trip that I need a new outfit for. There's the 8th grade luncheon that I need a new outfit for. There's graduation itself which I already have my dress for [mom, D'asia, and I went shopping for it the moment it looked promising that graduating was even in my future]. There's the after graduation family dinner that I so cannot show up to in the same clothes I walk across the stage in, and therefore need a new outfit for.

And then there's the post 8th grade party that it's rumored that Demitry Haggardy is throwing at the end of summer. It's all the Arthur Ashe graduating class has been talking about lately. This is where my mind is focused when Mrs. Parker calls on me to answer some scientific question that I probably wouldn't have the answer to anyway even if I had heard it.

"Alijah, I am waiting."

I jerk to attention. What did she ask?? I dart my eyes from left to right, hoping to get a clue from somewhere. All eyes are on me and of course none are trying to assist. I strain slightly to see Erika who's holding up her notebook and pointing at something I can't see [she's such a smarty pants] because stupid Chauncey Denton is blocking her and on purpose. I know 'cause he's smirking at me while he's doing it.

"Ms. McKenna," Mrs. Parker says, addressing me again. "Eyes on me. Now, what is the answer?"

"I...I'm sorry. I didn't hear the question."

Mrs. Parker closes her eyes and shakes her head gently in that way that adults do to say they are so disappointed in you. She sits her chalk down and walks toward my desk. All the boys like her. They think she's just such a honey. I disagree. Her head is shaped like a light bulb and her nose is like the shape of an arrow. But she does have gorge green eyes and the bottom of a video vixen [not at all appropriate for a teacher. There should be a clause in the her contract or something forcing her to shrink it].

She reaches her finger toward my desk and before I realize what she's doing and react to stop her, she has the piece of notebook paper I'd been thoughtlessly scribbling on. My heartbeat speeds up just a bit as she glances it over.

"So, this is what has you so distracted that you can't answer my question."

"I'm sorry. I'll…uhm, just ask…me…" my voice fades though IDK Y. Nerves I suppose.

"Since you don't seem to be all that interested in what Newton had to say, maybe you'd like to tell the class what you find to be more educational."

I swallow hard and glance around. My eyes pick up on the smirk on Demitry's face and I turn back to Mrs. Parker quickly. My voice is hardly audible when I answer, "I'd rather not."

"Oh, yes. I would love to know more about…what is this? How to get an invite to Demi-"

I jump from my seat so fast you could swear I have rockets strapped to my ankles. I snatch the paper from her hand. I hadn't meant to do that. I only want to stop her from completely humiliating me. She's so lame. But I did it. I snatched it and she's none too happy.

"Well, class, it would seem Ms. McKenna is beyond my scope of authority and believes it acceptable to snatch things from the hands of her teachers."

"I…I don't…" I look over to Erika who shakes her head gently and gives me this look of empathy. Reluctantly and against my will, my eyes go back to the side of the room where Demitry and flunkie #1, Mya, are seated laughing at me just high enough that the kids around them are entertained but low enough that it doesn't threaten Mrs. Parker's coveted sense of authority.

Mrs. Parker hands the paper back to me and folds her arms across her chest which, unfortunately for her being a card carrying adult of normal height, is no bigger than mine. I think I'm headed back to my seat but clearly I'm wrong. "Why don't you take this to Mr. Fitzgerald and explain exactly what it has to do with Newton and/or Science in general."

I pause in front of my desk, rolling my eyes so far to the back of my head that for a sec I'm so afraid that they're gonna get stuck. I think how this is completely unfair and I cannot wait until I don't have to see "Light Bright" any longer!

"Any day now, Ms. McKenna," Demitry volunteers. "Some of us wanna learn."

"Really. Too bad some of you aren't capable of such a thing," I reply thoughtlessly. I immediately regret it, for now I'll never get an invite and I absolutely have to go to this party. Everyone that's anyone will be there.

"Alijah," Mrs. Parker scolds. "As a matter of fact, go straight to Principal Bellamy."

"But-"

"Now."

"This is so unbelievable. Demitry can just say whatever she wants and I get sent to the Principal's office."

"Alijah."

"Too bad she's graduating. Now you'll have to find someone else to tell you how to do your job." Okay, now I know I've gone too far. But if I'm going to the Principal, it better be for good reason.

"Alijah McKenna, out. Now!"

Most of the class snickers and a few outright laugh, and I

could just die right here. Right on the spot. But I don't. Instead I straighten my spine and stand as tall as possible, grab my books and shove them inside my backpack before turning away wordlessly and walking toward the classroom door en route to discuss my insubordination with ol' Joe, the Principal. I've spent so much time with him we should be on a mutual first name basis.

Princi-pal. I wonder why they spell it that way, different from principle. Yeah, he's no pal of mine. Before I leave I hear Demitry add: "I feel for her. Must be hard being the only Little Person in the entire 8th grade class."

The class roars with laughter. Most of them. I'm certain Erika doesn't find a thing funny, just as I'm certain Demitry will not be joining me on this little impromptu excursion despite her insensitive and potentially hurtful commentary.

I leave before our science teacher issues her idle threat to the class. No one but my friends believe me but I swear most of the teachers at Arthur Ashe treat me harsher because of Auntie Nay. They're so concerned with the other students not feeling that I get some sort of special treatment that they actually treat me completely unjust. It would be so terribly humorous if it wasn't so infuriating, but Demitry actually *does* get special treatment just 'cause her mom is the stoopid superintendent.

I'm halfway to the principal's office before I realize that I didn't wait around long enough to get a hall pass. Stephie Sinclair is on duty. You should know something about me, I'm not an unreasonable person and I don't just not like peeps for the thrill of it. But Stephie Sinclair is like maggots crawling under your skin so you need laser treatment to get rid of 'em.

She begins her stroll in my direction, a smug look already

consuming her freckled face. Her red hair is split in two perfectly neat braids, not a strand out of place. Her brown rimmed, cat eye frames sit too high on her long nose [never mind that she is much too young for cat eye frames]. And the plaid skirt she wears can stand to be a couple inches longer to conceal her knobby knees.

"Hall pass."

Ugh. "I don't have one, Stephie. I'm going to the office."

"You need a hall pass."

"Well, I don't have one. Sorry. Mrs. Parker is sending me to deliver a message to Principal Bellamy and she was kinda busy and forgot to give me a hall pass."

"That will be one demerit."

"What? I just – OMG. You're such-"

"Shall I make it two?"

"Just give me the demerit. Please." I add the nicety to satisfy her ego. Maybe she'll let me go faster.

"Name."

My head jerks and I tilt it sideways and my eyes go up to meet hers. "You're kidding me right?"

"Name."

"Stephie, c'mon. We've gone to the same school for like, all our lives."

"Name."

I sigh. "Alijah."

"Spell that."

"Really, Stephie? I need to go, like now." I begin to walk away and continue the normally quick trek to the office.

"Go and I'll just deliver 3 demerits to Mrs. Drake. That's an automatic detention," Stephie calls after me but I keep walking.

"You don't even know my name, so why do I care?"

"Fine. Detention it is for you, Alijah McKenna."

Heat rushes all the way from my toes, throughout my body and my cheeks are now hot. Now here's a science topic. You can fry an egg on my face. How is it that one little gap toothed Svengali has the ability to do such a thing to me physically [and by the way, Auntie Nay should be so totally proud that I even remembered that a Svengali is some evil jerk that manipulates another into doing what they want]?

I stalk back in her direction and reach for the demerit while biting my lip so hard that I actually draw blood, but I have to in order to prevent saying anything that could make matters worse.

"Name."

"Alijah McKenna," I say through gritted teeth.

"Spelling."

I exhale heavily but respond. After she jots my name down and stretches her arm in my direction, it takes everything in me not to snatch the demerit. I force a smile on my face and politely remove the piece of paper. I turn away silently and walk the remaining distance to the office.

I push into the office, actually relieved to be away from science and Stephie Sinclair. That is until –

"Ali? Why aren't you in class?"

"Auntie N – I mean, Mrs. Jackson. I – I…" Really, dude? This is where my day is headed?!

"You, you what? Ann, where is this child supposed to be right now? Clearly she done picked up a stutter and can't answer a simple question."

The office admin, Mrs. Ann Drake, to my horror, responds in the honesty that I was trying to avoid. "Right up in here, Nay. Amelia called and told me to expect her and send her in to Principal Bellamy."

"What? For what this time?"

"Chile, what else?"

I swallow the lump in my throat. And then the other lump and try not to get caught sending death rays from my eyes to Mrs. Drake.

"That mouth of yours is gonna get you in some trouble you can't get yourself out of some day."

"But I didn't do anything, Aunt – I mean, Mrs. Jackson."

"Mmhm."

"I swear."

"Mmhm. Amelia Parker is just picking on you, I know."

"But she is!"

At this moment, Principal Bellamy steps out the office and I am summoned.

"Don't try to convince me that Mrs. Parker sent you out for no good reason. Explain it to your momma when you get home tonight."

My eyes widen as Auntie Nay grabs her stack of papers, waves goodbye to Mrs. Drake, and walks out the office without another word to me.

"Ali McKenna," the principal bellows.

I inhale deeply and trudge his way.

Family Bizzyness 💜

My bed is moving in perfect rhythm beneath me. I roll from my belly and onto my back, bringing my cush pillow with me. I lay for a moment longer, just hoping that it'll stop on it's own. It does not.

"Maddie," I say. But granted, there's a frog in my throat so huge I'm sure it has warts. "Maddie."

The bouncing continues and the bed dips sporadically in different places. "Awi."

I snatch the pillow from my face and slam it at my side. I love my little brother very much – but not always at the same level. "Maddex! Oh my God!"

The jumping ceases. "Oooh."

"Alijah Dominique!" That voice belongs to my mother, who yells from some unknown place in the hall just beyond my room.

"I'm sorry."

But my apology doesn't register and quickly her frowned face is in my doorway. "What have I told you about taking our Lord's name in vain? What does he have to do with what you have going on in here?"

"But, Mom, Maddie keeps-"

"You and that mouth of yours. I swear, little girl. You're gonna get enough. You're already grounded for talking back to Mrs. Parker.

Don't make me add on to your sentence."

And then she's off to tend to whatever it was she was doing when she somehow managed to hear my plea to Father God above for peace. And there's Maddex again. Bounce. Bounce. Bounce. I grab the pillow and cover my face once more.

"Aaaaaaaaaarrrrrgh!!!!"

"Fix. Me. Some. Eggs. Fix. Me. Some. Eggs. Fix-"

"Tell Mom to make you eggs," I say, except it's really muffled and since he can't understand he insists that I repeat myself. I toss the pillow away. "Moooooom! Maddie wants eggs!"

"He asked you, didn't he?" She calls from the end of the hall.

"I. Asked. You. I. Asked. You."

I sit up in bed, all set to grill him until he gets intimidated enough to change his mind. But he's just too cute. Annoying. But really cute. I catch him mid jump and pull him to me. He's laughing and squirming cause I'm tickling his little rib cage. I stop and he calms though he's still breathing pretty hard.

I pull his face back and look into his eyes. Mine are crossed and he laughs. "Why didn't you ask Millie? She makes better eggs than me."

"No," he says, almost disgusted by the idea. I feel a little proud about that. "She ain't here."

"Alijah, correct him," Mom yells. How does she hear everything?

"She's not here," I say.

"She no here," Maddex repeats.

I sigh and gently push him away as I tumble to the edge of the bed. I sit for a moment processing that I'm awake at...uhm, 9:15 on a Saturday morning. My naked toes feel around for my brand new Nick & Nora monkey slippers. They're so completely the hotness. I stand and grab Maddie's hand, leading him out of my room. As we pass by D'asia's room, I hear the tap-tapping of keys. I could care less what she's working on. Probably her friggin' college thesis for all I know.

"Mornin', D," I grumble in passing.

"D'asia and good morning." She hates to be called simply by her initial. Generally I'm respectful but mornings like this, who cares?

"Well, look who done joined the land of the living. Good morning, Squirrel."

PAUSE! You were not supposed to hear that! Grrr.... Fine. Yes. Squirrel. That's the nickname my family decided was so befitting of me. Actually it's a name my Poppa [aka my granddad] gave me when I was a kid because I was so small. They hardly ever use it anymore anyhow because they know I hate the name, unless Poppa is the one saying it, of course. But this isn't Poppa standing in my kitchen. It's my new uncle Parker Greene, Tee Tee Yashi's most recent husband. I don't know who gave him a pass to call me Squirrel, and I don't like it.

I use the refrigerator door as a shield and try not to get caught rolling my eyes. "Hey, Uncle Park."

"Ya mama say you graduating."

"Yep. Next week," I say, faking enthusiasm. I'm excited but not really trying to have this conversation with the old guy.

"Ooh, chile. I can't hardly believe you old enough to be anywhere near wearing somebody cap and gown. Yo' l'il teeny self."

I cringe. I've given a pass to Uncle Park cause he hasn't been around long but the novelty of my size really should have worn off by now. I grab the eggs and butter from the 'fridge and try hard not to slam them on the counter.

"Uncle Park, no disrespect intended but can you please not call me teeny."

"Why? You are."

These aren't Uncle Park's words. I turn toward the open back door where Millie is walking through. She's in sweats and one of her boyfriend's varsity tees, with her hair pulled back in a rough ponytail [which I'm so sure she did on purpose because it's so incredibly oxymoronic like buying brand new used jeans].

"Shut up, Millie. You don't even know what's going on in here."

"Oooh, Awi say, shet up Miwwi," says Maddex.

"Mom," Millie cries out.

"Oh my gosh, Millie, you're such a tattle."

"Mom, Ali's talking trash to me!"

"Am not," I scream.

"Ma. Awi say, shet up Miwwi."

My eyes bulge in Maddie's direction. I'm cooking him breakfast, he's supposed to be #teamalijah. Where's the loyalty around here? Millie laughs and walks out the kitchen after greeting Uncle Park who just looks way too amused by the entire scenario.

"Alijah! Whatever is going on down there, cut it out!"

"Ugh! I didn't even do anything. Uncle Park, can you please tell her Millie started it?"

He just laughs. "Uhn uhn, Squirrel. I learned a long time ago don't get in family business."

"But you're family."

"My name Bennet and I ain't in it."

"Ugh! So unfair."

"Awi say, shet up Miwwi."

I close my eyes tight and shake my head, quietly counting down the years until I can leave this place.

 Graduation Day

Today is my day. Finally, it's here.

"Alijah, hurry up in there. Other people need to get ready. I swear you gonna be late to your own funeral." I hear my mom fidgeting on the other side of the bathroom door. I suppose she's combing D'asia's hair 'cause I here her complaining. D'asia is tender-headed, partly because her hair is so thick. The other part is because she's too lazy to comb it properly.

It's my day.

"For goodness sake, Ali, will you please get out the bathroom! I need to flat iron my hair, else I'm not going to this stupid thing," Millie calls out.

"You're going, Millicent," Mom says.

"Not if my hair looks like this."

"Millie, you're going."

"Ugh, she's such a lame."

I listen to the sound of Millie stalking away. My day.

"I got go potty. Ma, ma! I got go potty."

"Maddie-honey, you have to wait. Ali's in the bathroom."

"But I got go potty."

"Then tell Ali to hurry out of the bathroom."

"A-wi! I got go potty, now!"

"Alijah-"

"Be out in a minute," I lie. I'm not doing anything. Just standing in front of the mirror staring at my reflection. Today is my last day as a grade schooler. I'll take as much time as I feel I need.

"Goodness. Okay, Maddie, go in Mommy's room and knock on my bathroom door and tell daddy you have an emergency." I hear his little feet take flight. "D'asia, you come with me. I'm sure Millie's got something in that beauty salon of hers that can tame this mess."

I listen as they depart. My smile broadens. Yep, it is so my day.

"Aliiiiiii," Simone squeals as soon as I walk into the auditorium. A broad smile breaks out on my face and I rush in her direction and we hug tight.

"Where's Erika?"

Simone points to Erika who couldn't look less enthusiastic about the day if she tried. She heads our way. Simone places her thick palms firmly on her hips and tilts her head slightly as she watches Erika on the approach. I stand beside her, my arms folded across my chest and lips twisted.

I know that we look odd standing here. Simone is tall. She's like, 5'5" [5'7" in her moms pumps she's wearing] and we still have another 4 years of growing to do. She's very beautiful with her slanty brown eyes and new pageboy cut that reaches just beyond the cap she's wearing.

"Why does she look so miserable?" I ask just as Erika reaches us.

"I do not look miserable."

"You totally look miserable," says Simone.

"I'm fine. I just wanna get this over with."

Erika looks beautiful, too. Her gown is open and I can see the pretty purple knee-length dress and small pearls around her neck. Classy and classic. Her hair is pinned to the side of her head with a purple flower attached. She's taller than me [everyone is taller than me] but not as tall as Simone.

I grab her wrist and pull her nearer to us. "It's graduation day. Oh. Em. Gee. You should be so psyched. Arthur Ashe, no more. Wilma Rudolph, here we come."

Erika loses her battle with faux negativity and gives up a smirk. "I'm happy, guys. Of course. I just…this ritual…I don't feel like sitting here forever while some pompous jerk drones on about all the wonderful lessons learned here at Arthur Ashe Elementary and Junior High."

"Aahhh," Simone and I sigh in unison.

"Aahh, what? What is that supposed to mean?"

Simone glances at me for support before speaking. "Aren't you, like, totally one of those pompous speech giving…jerks?"

My eyes widen and I nudge her in the ribs with my elbow. "Simone."

"Well. Her words, not mine."

Erika frowns. "If you're implying that I'm upset because Toby Carter beat me out for valedictorian-"

"No, no...never," we lie.

"I told you before, I could care less. It's just a stupid title. Besides, he only got it because I was out for two weeks thanks to stupid appendicitis. And I'm still salutatorian, so it's fine."

"Guys. Guys."

"What is it, Simone?" I inquire.

Her teeth are gritted when she responds. "Look who is headed this way."

I shrug, then pause because I see him. I totally see him and I have no idea what he's doing here, but I take a wild guess. Gage Campbell is walking directly toward us. I glance around. It must be a mistake, maybe he's going to see someone else. He hardly spoke to us when he attended Arthur Ashe, why would he approach us now? But to my right is Simone and on my left is Erika and I see no one else but Mom and Mrs. Toledo [D'asia's homeroom teacher] chatting several steps away.

"Is he coming for us?" Simone asks under her breath. "Oh my gosh, oh my gosh. Gage Campbell is approaching us. What do I look like? Is my makeup okay?"

"Shhh," Erika scolds. "He's just a stupid boy, and why are you wearing makeup anyway?"

"It's graduation day. Duh."

We're standing in a row with me low center, trying to be discreet but we must look so obvious in our ogling. "Will you guys be quiet," I mutter as my mind drifts off into fantasy land. In my world, Gage is walking toward us in slow motion. There's a crazy blur filter around him cause, duh, nothing is more important in this moment than he is. He's flashing his killer smile and perfect white teeth [his Pops is a dentist]. He is so uber-fashionable, moreso now that he's in high school.

He's in front of us now. His mouth is moving but I don't know what he's saying. I don't really care. I only watch his mouth and those teeth and now his gorgeous brown eyes and back to his teeth. Now he's looking at me directly. No one else matters. Not Simone. Not Erika. Not Demitry Haggardy who he dated until he graduated last year and decided it would be best for them to not try to sustain, what he referred to as, a long distance relationship, though I'm pretty sure she's the reason he's even at our graduation.

His mouth is moving and since no sound is coming out I do my best to read his lips. He says…I…love…you…I love you! "Me too," I sigh.

Erika glances down and nudges me hard. Then Simone does the same. I jerk back to reality. Oh my gosh! What have I said? What have I done? I glance panicked between the two of them, then swallow the lump in my throat before focusing on Gage again.

He chuckles, a look of utter confusion on his face. "Yea, alright. Maybe I'll see you guys around." And like that, he's gone.

Simone and Erika wave goodbye. Me? I'm way too embarrassed to make a move. Once the distance is safe, they both turn to face and hover above me. Never before have I actually felt my height so much.

"What was that?" Simone questions.

"I don't…I don't know. Oh my gosh, what did he say?"

Erika answers, "He said you look nice today."

I panic. "And what did I say?"

Simone answers, "Me too."

Oh the horror! Me too? Gage Campbell told me that I look nice and I answered, me too?!

And as if she can sense I did something stupid, Millie walks past and says, "Dork."

"Ignore her," Erika tells me.

"Yea, sure," I whisper. I'll ignore my sis but Demitry Haggardy is shooting darts in my direction with her eyes. How do I ignore her? I may not like her, but I need to be invited to her party. I shrug it off and head to my seat as the graduation is called to order. This is my day. Nothing will ruin it for me. Okay, so yes, I just made a bit of a fool of myself. But still. My day.

D'asia rushes behind me just as I'm about to take my place and whispers in my ear. "Guess what? Mrs. Toledo set up a meeting for next week with Principal Bellamy, mom and me."

"That's great, D'asia. I'm proud of whatever new accomplishment you achieved but can we discuss it later? I'm kinda about to graduate," I whisper back.

"I know, I know. I'm sorry. It's just that, I think I'm getting promoted."

"Yea, D'asia, straight A's. You'll get promoted to the 8th grade like you get promoted every year."

"No. Promoted to 9th grade. I think I'm going to high school with you."

I turn to face her and my rear misses the chair. I squeal in pain when I hit my knee on the back of the chair in front of me and catch a glimpse of Ruda LeGuin scowling at me as I crash to the floor and Kyle McKenzie laughs. I turn around and scowl at him before refocusing on D'asia. "You're what?" I ask much louder than I intended.

"I'm going to high school with you next year," she repeats and dances away, all smiles and good cheer.

And just like that, my life is over.

Summer Camp

 Chi Gurl

My life is officially over, Reilly. Over!"

I'm sitting on the step just below my friend Reilly Johansson. I'm planted between her legs with my head tilted firmly against her left knee while she's using a fine tooth comb to create the perfect part in my hair.

"Girl, you are being way melly."

"Me, melly? Really? For really, really? No, I don't think so. Considering the serious nature of the event that has transpired, I think my reaction is pretty legit."

"Keep still." She pops my head gently and I stop moving. "Yeah, girl, really. Y'all ain't phenna be in the same classes or nothin', right?"

"No, we won't be in the same classes. She's going to be in AP classes while I'm in regular ed classes. As if it isn't enough that Millie's still there."

"You will be okay. Y'all gone run in different circles, be in different classes. Wilma Rudolph is a pretty big school, you prolly won't even run into either one of your sisters. Just chill."

"Chill," I repeat.

"Yes, girl. Chill."

"Yeah, well, you wouldn't be saying that if you were going to high school and Kelly was going with."

Reilly pauses to ponder this logic. "Yeah. You prolly right. But it ain't about me, it's about you."

Reilly is pretty new. She moved to Eden Grove from Chicago just over a year ago. She's two years younger than Simone, Erika, and me and she couldn't be any more different. I think that's why I like her because she's nothing like me or anyone that I know. Simone agrees. Reilly has thee biggest crush on my GBFF [guy best friend forever], Justin. I don't think he cares about her one way or another. Erika can't stand Reilly, and Reilly is less than tolerant of Erika.

Erika swears that Reilly is fake. She doesn't talk like us but more like a character off any cliché urban flick on TV or in theatres past and present. And she ends nearly every sentence with, *girl*. She says she's from a place called East Rogers Park. Every time the two argue, she always says, "Don't blame me. I'm just a product of my environment" which leaves us with the vision of her environment as being someplace in the heart of some urban jungle with gun slinging and chalk outlines but she says it's not like that. That it just is what it is.

IDK. I don't think Reilly's fake and I really like her. But she doesn't understand what I'm dealing with. She's the firstborn of three and she is very much in charge. Kelly and Brock don't give her any trouble as far as I can tell.

"Here comes your girl," Reilly says, distracting my thoughts. I glance up to see Erika crossing the street, the wind blowing her honey-blonde tinted 'fro into varying poses. Reilly exhales and her voice softens, practically dances. "And your guy."

I wave to Erika and Justin. Like I said, Reilly has the biggest crush on Justin but he's not hardly interested. He actually has the hugest crush on Erika but she's so not into him. She's like D'asia but less genius and could only get into Justin if he was a book. Besides, she's saving her love for Khalil Hamlin, Ms. Davina Hamlin's only son. He's handsome and uber-intelligent, and Erika is head-over-heels in love with him. The moment she found out he was headed to medical school every other guy was spoiled for her.

He's not in her league, at all. As a matter of fact, he just left last week to get settled in at college. But she has a plan. Work really hard in her AP classes at Wilma Rudolph, do summer extra credit courses and night school during her junior year so she can graduate early, skipping her senior year entirely and going right into college – the same one Khalil attends. She'll be a freshman and he'll be a senior. They'll meet again and he'll realize she's not a little girl anymore. The two will fall madly in love and together build a medical empire. He'll be whatever she thinks he's gonna be, and she'll be the most sought after cardiothoracic surgeon in the country [like the female version of Dr. Burke from those Grey's Anatomy reruns she loves so much, the reason for her chosen profession].

Justin enters the gate and playfully pops the side of my head before taking a seat on the bottom step. "What up, Big Head?"

"Quit it, Justin. You play too much."

Erika pauses and stares at me, speaking with her eyes. She's asking why I'm letting Reilly mess with my hair. I'm telling her to mind her own. Her eye roll implies that she's sorta miffed that I didn't come to her to braid my hair. I twist my mouth and send the response that she's always too busy and I didn't want to wait. What I don't say via body language or otherwise, is that Reilly does a much better job anyhow. Her braids are tighter, last longer, and they don't give me a headache like most other peoples do. Reilly's dream is to be hairstylist to the stars. I think she'll make it come true.

Reilly tosses an auburn braid behind her shoulder and pushes my head to the other side. "What up, Erika?"

"Hello, Reilly. Ali, call me when you're done."

"Are you kidding me?" I ask, astounded.

"I'll be home."

"Erika."

"What?" Our eyes lock, quietly competing for dominance. I win. She exhales heavily but passes through the gate and takes a seat opposite Justin.

"Hi, Justin," Reilly sighs, now completely distracted from the task of making me look presentable.

He nods, barely looking up from whatever game he's playing on his phone. "Hey."

"You look cute today."

"Thanks."

"I mean, you always look cute but today you just look extra cute. Is that a new shirt?"

"Nope."

"Oh. Cause I just ain't never seen it before so I thought it was new."

"Reilly," Erika begins, "do you presume to have seen every shirt in the boy's closet?"

"No. I ain't say that."

"Didn't say that. You didn't say that."

"I ain't say that and you shouldn't presume to be able to correct me. Whatever. Y'all are so uptight out here. This place is alright but I swear y'all need to just relax. You, Miss Thing, need to relax."

"Excuse me?"

"You excused."

"You know what, you little - "

"Guys," I groan.

"Anyway," Reilly continues, "you thirsty, Justin? I made some Kool Aid. Berry Blue. Wanna glass? I can have my sister bring you one from my house. Kelly!"

"No thanks."

"You sure. We have cookies, too. I made chocolate chip cookies last night. They're so good. You should try one. Kelly!"

"I don't like chocolate."

"Oh."

An awkward silence falls around us. Suddenly, Erika jumps back to her feet and heads for the gate. "Call me when you're done."

"Erika," I call out.

"When you're done!"

I want to scold Erika but I can't blame her. Reilly gets pretty gushy where Justin is involved.

"You have really nice eyes," she says to him.

"Thanks."

"I want babies someday with eyes like that."

I think I'm gonna be sick.

Little Women

"Something's going on at your house," Simone says, as she runs up to me. "It looks like a party. You having a party and you didn't invite me? Loser."

A ginormous question mark forms on my face. "I'm not having a party."

"Someone's having a party. I went to your house looking for you. Jada answered and said you weren't there."

Jada is my cousin, by the way. Jadonna's daughter. I wait for Simone to finish but she doesn't. "Jada's there. And?"

"Why is Jada there?"

"I don't know. Maybe her mom is there. She's my cousin, she can be there."

"Well, there are like four cars in front of your house and I saw streamers on the wall."

"What?" I rush down the block toward my house with Simone in tow. I can hear Lady Gaga before I even reach the gate. I rush through, tossing my soccer ball on the lawn before jogging up the steps and pulling the screen door toward me. The front door is open wide. I stop abruptly and look around. There are streamers on the wall like Simone said. On the far right wall there is a huge, shimmery banner that says, Congratulations. I look up and see Aunt Jaclyn standing on a stepladder taping tampons to the ceiling.

"You guys are so weird," Simone mumbles, a look of contempt on her face.

"No, no, no."

Aunt Jaclyn addresses me but I rush past and up the stairs, charging past Millie who is coming out the bathroom as I'm heading to D'asia's room.

"Hey, dwarf. Watch it."

"Not now, Millie."

She pauses and laughs. "Oh, I get it. You saw the tampons and you're upset because your little sister became a woman before you. Priceless."

I stop abruptly and turn to face her. Millie's standing there in a short, pink terry cloth robe and matching slippers. She exfoliated. I can tell because her cheeks are rosy. The pink makes me want to slap her but I just know Mom will intervene.

"Please don't tell me that this a Graduation Party."

"Duh. I'm sure the tampons are already dangling from the ceiling. You've been to enough to know the signs. Not one of your own but, well, maybe you'll be lucky enough to have one when you grow into your big girl body."

"Aaargh!" I charge at Millie. I don't think about it first and yeah, so what, she's taller than me. But I'm stronger than her. Pretty girls don't play sports and they surely don't lift weights. They play with boys and lift a mascara brush.

"Let go of me, you imp!"

"What is going on? Simone, you're just standing by while they fight?" Asks Mom.

"Sorry, Mrs. C. It's family stuff. I hate to get in the mid of these two. My eye. Remember."

She's referring to the one time she tried to break up a fight between Millie and me, and one of us socked her in the eye. Not on purpose. Total accident but, well, her eye was blackened for two whole weeks. She vowed to never intervene again.

I feel my body being pulled in one direction while someone grabs Millie and pulls her in the opposite direction. Millie's face is completely flushed and her damp hair is all over her head, some of it sticking to her face. She adjusts her robe and pulls the belt tight. For the first time I recognize that it's Laurence holding Millie up. Aunt Jaclyn rushes in and takes over keeping her away from me. Laurence throws his palms up in defeat and walks over to me and Mom. He tells her that he and Maddie are leaving, kisses her on the cheek and wishes her good luck with the party.

Out the blue we're surrounded by family that I hadn't even realized was there. Female cousins and aunts all look on in amusement, shame, disappointment, entertainment. D'asia finally emerges and tries to find out what the fight is about. I only glare at her.

"Mom, she's a psycho," Millie cries out. "She just attacked me for no reason."

"I had a reason! She antagonized me."

"Did not."

"Did too."

"I did not!"

"She knew exactly what she was doing. I hate her."

"Alijah," mom scolds.

Hot tears stream from my eyes. "I'm sorry but I don't like her very much." I pull out of my mother's grasp and push past D'asia, nearly knocking her over as I charge to my room, closing the door firmly [but careful not to slam it. Hey, I'm in enough trouble]. I collapse onto my bed and bury my face in my pillow. A scream that begins at my toes, churns through me and explodes into the downy softness.

There is a soft knock on my door. "Go away!"

"Ali. Can I come in?"

It's Simone. I sigh and slowly pull myself to seated. I smear my tears away with the backs of my hands. "Come on."

Simone is wrapping up a call on her celly as she crosses the threshold to my room. She closes the door behind and drops the phone in her purse. She walks carefully toward me, like she's afraid if she moves too fast I'll attack her next. She's wearing a black tutu, leggings and Chuck Taylors. I don't know why it stands out to me in this moment. She's so totally her own person. "I called Erika. She's on her way. Hope it's okay."

"Of course. Thanks."

Simone takes a seat beside me and looks into my face. "Don't cry Ali-Cat." Note: She, Erika, and Justin are the only ones who call me that and totally in private. "Why is she getting a graduation party anyway? You're the one that graduated."

"It's not that kind of graduation party, Simone. It's...it's a woman party."

Simone shrugs. "What does that mean?"

My door bursts open and Erika rushes inside. "D'asia got her period?"

I nod. "And I got into a fight with Millie. I'm gonna be so grounded."

"Was it at least worth it?"

"Totally," Simone says. "She won. Millie got her butt kicked."

I smile and nod. I'll probably be on lock for a few days but it's so well worth it.

Erika sits on the opposite side of me and wraps her arm around my shoulder, pulling me into her arms. "Look at it this way. D'asia's going to have to deal with cramps, PMS, chocolate binging, tampons."

"Water weight gain, mood swings."

"All that. Being a woman actually kinda sucks. It's so not all its cracked up to be. Sometimes I wish I could just be a kid again."

I wipe the last remaining tear from the corner of my eye and let my head fall on Erika's shoulder. Simone takes my hand in hers. "Thanks guys. I don't know what I'd do without you."

"Be a complete mess," Erika tells me.

"Right," I laugh, feeling so much better.

Iniquity

The meaning of the Word of the Day is: gross injustice or wickedness. A violation of right or duty. What a coincidence.

My fav sport like, ever, is soccer. I've played it since I was just a kid. Coach Lowe came along during my 4th grade year and started up a mini league at Arthur Ashe and I was the first in line for tryouts. But I was a hardcore soccer-head way before and had no problem proving my worth and was even made team captain by unanimous vote that same day.

I fell in love with the game the first time I saw *Bend It Like Beckham* when I was 5 years old [and I say the first time because I've seen it like a million-trillion times since]. When Parminder Nagra's character, Jesminder, ran circles with the ball around those stupid boys, I knew what I wanted to do with the rest of my life.

I begged Daddy to buy me a ball just like hers. He was all worried about my being so small and was positive that I would get hurt. He promised me when I got bigger I could have one. Well, when I turned six, I was still small [and he was still concerned] but I was much more articulate. And after Justin saw *Beckham* and confirmed the pure awesomeness of the sport I so came to appreciate, it was inevitable. Daddy had to give in.

Justin and I started a mini league on the block long before the coach showed, and I've been kicking butt ever since. I look forward to playing in the Women's Professional League after high school, following in the foot traps of the likes of Marisa Abegg and Ramona Bachman, replacing her as the youngest player in the league.

The first step to getting there is soccer camp, which I've done every summer [one way or another] for the past 4 summers. But this year will be the greatest ever. Thanks to Coach, me and Justin managed to get partial scholarships to attend the Nike Vogelsinger Soccer Academy at the University of Cali in Santa Barbara! The opportunity is so totally unbelievable. We're gonna spend 3-weeks being trained by the best in like, the greatest state in the US!

Everything is covered except $500 + spending money and Mom promised, when the opportunity was presented, that I would be going. July 15th and me and my GBFF are out this piece! I can hardly wait!

The house is so quiet I can actually hear myself think. The bright sun streaming through my window is beckoning me to rise. What day is it? That's the thing about summer, you totally lose track of time. Wednesday. Today is Wednesday. I glance at my clock. 11:16. Mom and Laurence are at work and Maddie is at Aunt Vee's daycare. I yawn and rise, slipping into my house shoes before leaving my room. D'asia's door is open but her room is empty. I glance toward Millie's door as I approach the top of the stairwell. It's closed and her pink and baby blue DND [Do Not Disturb] sign hangs from the doorknob.

I creep down the stairs into the silent living space and see no sign of D'asia. First I think that maybe she went into work with my mother [mom's a legal secretary for Vance DeWitt and sometimes she has us girls go with to help her with some menial task, like filing]. But when I step into the kitchen, I see the back door propped open.

I go out onto our back porch and stare across the huge yard. The green blades of grass shimmer beneath the sunlight and soft wind rustles the leaves on our oak. I love summer. The smell of it. The sense of it. The warm feeling of the sun's rays on my skin. After making the rounds, my eyes fall on D'asia who is sitting at the picnic table near the oak, bent forward and writing furiously. Her back is to me but I picture the tip of her tongue poking out the side of her mouth like in those old Peanuts cartoons.

The morning is perfect and I'm really not ready to go back

inside yet, so I stroll across and take a seat beside my sister. She doesn't even notice my presence. She's completely intent on whatever geeky project she's working on. I say good morning, but she doesn't even hear me.

"Oh my gosh, D'asia. Hello?"

"Hunh? Oh, good morning, Sis."

I glance over her shoulder. Now I'm a little curious about what's so darn important. "What is that?"

"My application."

"Application for what?"

"Aunt Beverly told me about a special summer SEMAA program. To be considered, I have to get this off to her today."

Okay, I don't know about you unless you're on that uber-genius level like my sis, but I am so very confused. "See-mah?"

"S-E-M-A-A. It's an acronym. Stands for Science, Engineering, Mathematics and Aerospace Academy."

"Ahh, okay. I suppose. What's this for?"

"I just told you. Science, Engineering, Math-"

I shake my head in frustration. "No, I mean...well, I haven't heard you say anything about some summer science school."

"Well I didn't know about it until yesterday and we missed the application deadline, but Aunt Beverly knows someone at the NASA program who can push mine through if I get it to her soon enough."

So I didn't know what SEEMA was but I certainly know what NASA is and the sound of this is making my head spin. I've never heard of a NASA program in Eden Grove, which means she must have to travel to get to their little space school. And my Aunt Bev [my dad's sister] lives in El Paso, Texas which means, at the very least, airfare.

"Sooo, it's a school, right? Like summer school?"

D'asia fills in another box as she responds to me. "Yes, Ali. It's a school."

"So then it's free." I feel relief. School equals free and airfare can't cost all that much in the summer time.

She chuckles sarcastic-like and I instantly have a migraine. "Not hardly. I told you, it's a special program. A very special program that runs for 6 weeks, so participants have to pay a tuition."

The world is turning and right about now, it's getting harder and harder to hold on. Tuition? But how much could it be? Not much, right? It's school. You can't charge too much for summer school. $50? $75?

"I will spend the summer living with Aunt Bev and Uncle Deke," she continues unprompted, like she's been hoping someone cared enough to give her a chance to talk about this stuff out loud. "But the tuition has to be covered up front."

I lean closer to get a better look at the form she's filling in, and there in a bold black box it reads: *Tuition cost $750. Non-refundable registration fee $300. Make check or money order payable to...*

SEVEN HUNDRED FIFTY DOLLARS!

"No," I say, jumping up from the bench. "No. Way."

"What's the problem? You act like you're the one paying for it," D'asia says, but I don't respond because I already know what she is clearly oblivious to or unconcerned with – in a sense, I likely am. I run straight back indoors and to the portable phone that's sitting on the counter.

I dial my mother's work number and launch into an all out verbal assault the second I hear: "Vance Dewitt's office. Bernadette speaking. How may I help you?"

"Please tell me it isn't so, Mom. Please. Please, Mom."

She's hesitant to respond and I can hear it. I caught her off guard but I don't care. Not my concern. I just need to know that I'm not getting bumped for D'asia and her space odyssey. Not again. Not this year. Of all years, not this one.

"I suppose D'asia told you."

"Not exactly. Mom...don't..."

"Alijah, sweetheart. Please. Can we discuss this when I get home this evening?"

"No. Mom, no. I need to discuss this now."

She pauses as if to consider my demand. "Fine. I'm sorry, honey. I've run the numbers over and over but we just can't afford to pay for both you girls this summer."

"Then pay for mine. I asked first. Mine is more affordable. I'm older!"

I can hear the empathetic smile through the phone line and I cringe. I hate when she does that. Empathy. That was once the Word of the Day and suddenly in this moment I recall its definition: the intellectual identification with or vicarious experiencing of the feelings, thoughts, or attitudes of another. If she was truly empathizing with me, she'd never allow D'asia's last minute plans to ruin my long-term ones.

But instead she says, "It isn't that simple. This is a very unique and incredible opportunity for your sister. This chance may not come along again. Your aunt and uncle are stepping in to help make this happen. They're going to cover her airfare and provide food and board all summer long, but I can't expect them to pay her tuition as well."

"Why not? They don't have any children of their own to pay for. And besides and more important, you promised me."

"Alijah, don't be unreasonable."

"Unreasonable?" Tears I hadn't before realized had formed, are now filling up my throat, making it difficult to speak in coherent sentences. "What about me? I earned a scholarship, Mom. Coach went through a lot to make this happen for me. And now...I just have to...forget about it? When were you gonna tell me? There's not enough time for me to even try to raise the funds!"

"Listen, sweetie. I'm sorry. I really, truly am. I wish we could afford to send both you girls away this summer but we can't. I had to make the hard choice. That's what parenting is all about, making the hard choices. For you Ali, it's just a game. I know you love it but it's just a game that you'll outgrow in a few more years. For D'asia, this is her future. Sometimes we have to make sacrifices for the greater good. You should feel honored to do this for your little sister.

"Now, honey, I really have to get back to work. I'm very sorry, really I am. It seems like the end of the world now but by summer's end, you won't even remember this conversation. I love you. We'll talk more when I get home."

And like that, she's gone, along with my plans, goals, hopes and dreams for *my* future. When does anyone ever care about what I want to do with *my* future? A future that revolves around me and this so-called "game".

Lemon Laws

☠ Nice Satan

om, Laurence, and Aunts Jaclyn and Rene all piled inside our SUV and escorted D'asia to the airport. Mom begged me to come with cause she was under the impression that I needed to show solidarity with my sister by seeing her off. According to Mom, D'asia felt guilty enough that I was suffering for her yet again. She claimed my insistence on staying home was punishing her more than she deserved [not that I truly believe that Mom thinks D'asia deserves any punishment]. I wasn't buying it and I wasn't about to concern myself with making her feel better about taking future food out of my mouth. If she felt so much guilt, why didn't she back out then? Hmpf.

So now she's in Texas spending the summer with Aunt Bev and Uncle Deke so she can attend this special SEEMA program. She's called me a couple times but I'm never available. Justin left for Cali two days after D'asia. He called me as soon as he got there and completely dumbed down the experience so I wouldn't feel bad.

He's been gone for a week and that was the only time I heard from him. It can't be all that bad in Santa Barbara.

So, in D'asia's absence, I've taken to becoming the complete and totally reclusive sibling. Partly because I can't stop crying long enough to function in the real world. The other part [and I would so deny this if accused] is to make sure that my mother suffers just as much as I am. I hope her conscious is killing her!

Erika and Simone spent the first night of Justin's departure with me but I haven't allowed them back. I really don't wanna see anybody. I hardly come out my room unless my stomach insists, and then I eat just enough to survive and it's back to the fortress of solitude, aka my bedroom, where I sit and stare out the window at the world passing me by.

This is where I am now, watching Reilly play a game of Double Dutch with my younger cousin Reide and the twins from two blocks over. There's a knock on my door first, then it opens. I don't budge or acknowledge my intruder.

"Mom says come and eat dinner," Millie says in a tone like it's my fault she had to come anywhere near me.

"Not hungry."

"Then you tell her. But she really wants you to eat and I'm so sure she's over your little pity party."

"Whatev."

There is quiet but Millie hasn't yet left. "That's it? That's all you gotta say? Whatev?"

"Yea, Millie. What do you want me to say? Gloat. Talk mess about me and my size. Talk crap because D'asia left and I have to stay here. In case you're having difficulty figuring it out, I don't really care."

I hear her shuffling about and next thing she's right beside me. "You're really upset, huh?"

"What do you think? I asked Mom about Vogelsinger months ago. Aunt Bev calls up out the blue talking about she's faxing an app and needs it back within 24-hrs and suddenly stupid D'asia has my soccer camp money. Yeah, I'm kinda upset."

"I feel you. But you're a beast at the sport already. Is it really that bad, you not getting to go?"

Did Millie just compliment me? Surely I must have misunderstood but right now, I don't really care to clarify. "She's a genius, Millie. Everyone knows it. Would it really have been that bad if *she* didn't go?"

Millie seems to contemplate this for a moment. "You've been locked in this room for a week. Your hair looks like a rats nest, you're ashy and pale, and if I'm not mistaken-" Millie leans forward and sniffs the air around me. I give her my most incredulous look and recoil, "-you smell."

"Whatever. I don't smell."

"When's the last time you took a shower?"

I try hard to form some words but it's a definite struggle. I jump up from my seat and walk to my bed. "That's not the point. How would you feel if you had some stupid ANTM style model camp you were invited to and you couldn't go?"

Millie twists her lip in contemplation. "It's like that?"

"Totally like that."

"Sorry," she says and it even sounds like she means it.

I mumble a thanks in response.

"You still have to eat though. And if you're trying to guilt Mom, it's not happening. She gave you a week. She's not going to be too much more patient."

"I'm not-"

"Don't try to sell me, little sister. Been there done that a hundred times before you were even old enough to see it as a viable option." Millie walks to my bedroom door but pauses and looks back. "Look, Isaiah is coming by in an hour or so to take me to a movie. You're welcome to come if you like. I mean, provided you bathe of course."

My brow arches like super high. I can't recall the last time my sister invited me to go anywhere and do anything with her and especially not with her *and* her boyfriend.

"What's the catch?"

"No catch. I still think you're an annoying little elfkin who shoulda been left at the hospital after birth. But, you are my sister and for once you have normal size people problems. Just trying to be supportive. Take it or leave it."

She exits without a response. I contemplate the offer, which is definitely a once in a decade sorta thing. It might be kinda nice to have a real sister right now. Maybe I need that. I exhale wearily as I pull my body from the bed and snatch my towel and robe off the back of my closet door.

🍦 Praline Ice Cream

I've been soooo looking forward to leaving Arthur Ashe and all the "little" jokes behind [most of which were initiated by Millie and passed down even after she was gone]. Being a freshman doesn't do much for being a petite girl, but it is supposed to give me an opportunity to recreate myself and take the focus off of my size and on me – Alijah McKenna. And although D'asia managed a last minute promotion, I'm still determined to make this work out for me.

For as much as I've been anxious about starting over at Wilma Rudolph High, Millie's been looking forward to her senior year. For more than being nearly done with her education in Eden Grove, it's an especially significant year because not only does she turn 17, she can finally – and I do mean, finally – get the car she's been dreaming of.

During the summer prior to her junior year, she boasted to everyone about how she was going to be driving to school come September. Her dad was on board and she figured that since she had her learner's permit, once she turned 16 and took her driving test, Mom could say nothing.

She couldn't have been more wrong.

Millie's not the brightest bulb on the Christmas tree. I take that back – kinda. She isn't unintelligent, just very pretty and since she learned that looks will open most doors, she became quite intellectually lazy. Mr. Torres was clueless about the slew of C's and D's on his only daughter's report card until Mom confronted him about his willingness to purchase a vehicle for an underachiever. Didn't he realize that a pretty car for a pretty girl who only cared about money, modeling, and cheering, wouldn't help her college apps?

Well, Millie was furious and terribly humiliated when the first day of school rolled around and she was forced to take the big yellow bus with the rest of her peers. Though I wanted to feel sorry for her, it was much too hilarious.

But Mom can't always be accused of being unreasonable. She made a deal with her eldest child. If Millie maintained a high C average for her entire Junior year, Yoan would be allowed to purchase her a vehicle for her next birthday. I've never seen my sister keep her nose so far in a book as the past year. Now the time has arrived. Her birthday is a month away, August 13th, and she is on a mission to find the perfect vehicle to pick her friends up in on the first day of school.

"This is it, Ali! I found it. The perfect, perfect car."

I turn away from the bowl of praline ice cream I'm eating with Erika and Simone, and see my sibling running my way, balancing a 13" laptop in her hands. Yea, yea, this is an odd sight. But I guess the whole experience of my younger sibling ruining my life struck a heart chord with my big sis, and it actually served to bond us.

Both of my friends look at me with utter confusion. I shrug and give my undivided attention to Millie who pushes my bowl away and sits the computer in front of me.

"It's perfect, Ali. Tell me it's perfect!"

I look at the image of the current model silver Mercedes Benz E550 Cabriolet with blood red interior. The top is dropped and a blonde looks thrilled to be inside of it. A twinge of jealously shoots through me but I push it away. I'm not even old enough to drive. Maybe we'll be rich by the time I am…though it's doubtful.

"It's…it's perfect. Simply perfect."

Erika and Simone gather around and look at the image in awe.

"OMG, Millie," Simone squeals. "I'm so completely green! You're def going to be the most popular girl in school with this car, hands down."

"I am the most popular, you rodent."

Simone sneers and shows Millie her tongue before returning her gaze to the car. Erika, who has completely lost interest, returns to her bowl of ice cream.

"Your mother is going to let you have a car like that when your sisters can never dream of having such a vehicle as their first?"

I glare at Erika. I know she's only trying to jab Millie for her snide comment to Simone but we're finally getting along and I don't need my friends ruining that for me. Whether I'll admit it aloud or not, I rather enjoy having a relationship with my sis. And besides, if I can keep this going it can only serve to improve my chances at a successful freshman year.

Fortunately Millie doesn't entertain the possibility. "It's not up to my mom, first of all. She said my dad could buy me a car if I kept my grades up. I did, so I can get – wait, why am I explaining anything to a crumb snatcher like you?" She turns away and heads to the stairwell but not before instructing me to make sure my "little freeloading friends clean up their mess before they leave."

Once she's out of earshot, I address Erika. "Why'd you have to say that?"

"Oh, please. You think I'm buying all this nice-nice big sister nonsense? She's so faux she should be picketed. As soon as you do or say something she doesn't like, or your mom denies her something, she's going to turn on you again."

"She might not."

"Yea, she will," Simone says through a mouthful of the good stuff.

"Whatever. You guys shouldn't be haters. You're supposed to be supportive."

"We are supportive," says Erika.

"So supportive," Simone seconds.

"Then act like it." I rise and take my bowl to the sink and rinse it before heading to the front door without them. I jog down the porch steps and stop at the front gate. I don't know why I'm so bugged out by their reaction to Millie and me actually getting along. I mean, it's probably never happened before and if it did it was during a time in history that I can't recall. I'm pretty sure they want me to be happy and don't mean anything by their reaction, but it still hurts my feelings nonetheless.

"Well, well, well, if it isn't Tiny Tim's midget sister."

I turn toward the voice to find myself face to...to...well, to boobs with Demitry Haggardy and the Lame Squad.

"Hi, Demi. How can I help you?"

"Well, I don't know, how *can* you help? Guys, how exactly can Ali McKenna help me?" She turns to face her drones, Mya and Kamahla Choudhary, who giggle like imbeciles. "If I need something off the top shelf, you can't get it. If I need a partner for the big girls ride at the fair, you can't get on. Let's see, what can you help me with, Ali? Certainly not my boyfriend, Gage. I don't need your help with that."

Now I am sooo baffled. "What are you talking about?"

"Just stay away from Gage, okay."

Sets of footsteps rush down behind me. "I think you're

confused," Erika says. "Gage Campbell is not your boyfriend, first of all. Secondly, so long as he stays away from us, we will be happy to stay away from that jerk."

"You don't know what you're talking about, you four-eyed geek. He's been my boyfriend since 6th grade."

Simone joins in. "And he dumped you in 7th."

"He didn't dump her," says Mya.

"Yea," Kamahla chimes in. "He just thought they needed a break since he was going to high school and couldn't be seen dating someone still in grade school. He, like, totally loves her but, oh my god, he moved on and she was still like a little kid-"

"Kam," Demitry squeals. Mya rolls her eyes and shakes her head as Kamahla mutters an apology.

"I wasn't dumped, okay. I didn't want to be with him until I came to Wilma Rudolph. You idiots have no idea what you're talking about."

I nod in feigned agreement. "Yeah. That makes lots of sense. Dumping your boyfriend right before he goes off to a world of older, smarter girls in wider variety. You're a genius, aren't you? *You* should be in AP classes."

I laugh and Erika and Simone join in.

"Like your kid sister?" Now Demitry has really hit a nerve. "Must suck to have to live in a household with two sisters that are better than you in every conceivable way. I wouldn't spend too much time stressing over it though. Life is too short. Oh, and so are you."

My eyes are slits and I don't blink for the longest time. The blur starts to make her head look like a soccer ball and it takes every ounce of inner strength for me not to run up and kick it.

"Oh," she continues from the street. "I hope your little nerd posse doesn't think they're getting an invite to my post 8th grade kickback. I wouldn't invite the three of you if my life depended on it!"

"And we wouldn't come if our lives depended on it," Simone calls out in response. Once Demitry, Mya, and Kamahla are far enough away she turns to us and says, "I so totally would go if my life depended on it. My life – our social life kinda does depend on it."

"Not mine," says Erika, taking a seat on the stoop. "I could care less about Demitry Haggardy, Mya Foster, Kamahla Choudhary, Gage Campbell, and any other stupid social climber from that circle."

"We're social climbers, aren't we?" Simone inquires.

"You are, sweetie. You are."

"Ali? We have to get invited to that party somehow. Our status entering high school will kinda depend on it. And who we are when we walk through the doors on day 1, is how we'll be perceived for the next four years." Simone reasons. I don't respond. I don't know what to think or say.

But Erika does. "Don't be ridiculous. I don't need those people. I'll survive just fine on my own."

"As an AP geek? Doubtful."

"Whatev. I'll be just fine. We'll all be."

I nod but I'm not so sure if it's actually in agreement or merely a reflex. I have Millie and D'asia working against me [socially and academically]. I have my height and lack of feminine development working against me. But Gage Campbell once said I looked nice [though I made a complete fool of myself when he did] and it's freaking Demitry Haggardy out, so it's sorta a big deal to me to be accepted by the pop kids. At this point, I don't really know what I feel.

◆ Birthday Girl

Today is thee big day.

Not for me, I'm not very likely to benefit. But then again, Millie and me have been kicking it with each other for the several weeks that D'asia has been gone. So maybe…just maybe I'll see myself passenger-side in her brand new Benz. That would definitely help my image in the event that Simone is right about the importance of how one enters high school.

But what would Erika and Simone say and how would they feel about it? Even if me and Millie somehow manage to become complete and total BSE's [Best Sisters Ever] that would have nothing at all to do with how she feels about those two. She would never have them in her new car. The remaining space will mos def be reserved for Laura and Lauren [the twins] and her closest bestee Genna. Gosh, how will I break the news to them?

I wake up late morning in Erika's bedroom to the feel of something wet and oddly smooth brushing against my face. I'm all scrunched up and trying to escape the weird sensation. When my eyes open, I find myself face to face with Bette Middleton, the Bellflower's Japanese Chin. Her big, round eyes set far apart, totally freak me out and I jump up, pushing her away.

"Ugh," I groan, wiping the wetness from my cheek. I swear she does this on purpose 'cause she knows I hate it.

Simone adjusts beneath the coverlet we shared, rolling over onto her left side. She smacks the slob between her lips a couple times before burying the side of her face deeper into the pillow. I shake off that disgusting display and swing my legs around to the floor beside Erika's guest bed and rise. I slip on one sandal, then drop to my knees and scrounge around for the other. Bette Middleton is there with me every step of the way.

I roll my eyes and feel relief when I find my right shoe, and slip it on. I don't wanna wake the girls so I creep quietly with Erika's dog hot on my trail. I'm nearly at the door when she yips at me.

"Shush." I glance back and verify that Erika and Simone are both sleeping soundly. I pull the door up gently behind me and head down the stairwell.

"Good morning, Ali. You leaving without breakfast?" Carolyn Bellflower, Erika's mom, is coming up from the basement holding a purple hamper firmly against her hip.

"Yeah. Today's Millie's birthday and Mom and Laurence are taking her to lunch and I gotta go with."

"Yes, that's right. Dette told me the other day. She's supposed to be getting a car, right?"

"Yep, a Benz."

"Mm. Dette is good. No way I would allow Erika to have a car that pricey for her first one. But I guess she knows what she's doing. Well, tell Millie I said happy birthday."

"I will," I say before heading out into the morning drizzle. I jog home, taking the back way, jumping the fence for our yard and entering through the kitchen. I'm completely caught off guard by what I witness.

"I cannot believe that you would do this to me," Millie screams, pacing back and forth.

I stop short, fearful of making my presence known. Mom is leaned against the sink, looking as though she's using everything inside of her to keep from spazzing out and ripping Millie a new one. I'm surprised to see Yoan Oliva-Torres in my kitchen, a sight rarely seen. He appears relatively calm, though a little anxious as he sits on a wooden stool in front of the countertop island. He lifts the mug in front of him and savors a sip of what's likely Mom's perfect coffee, completely unaffected as his daughter continues to pace and rant.

The only person to notice me is Laurence who is standing with his back to the wall and facing the doorway that I'm hesitant to pass through. His eyes are like saucers and I read his message loud and clear. I should leave and now. I step back without looking and my foot lands hard on one of Maddie's toys. I try to conceal my yelp but it doesn't work – I'm spotted.

"You." Millie walks my way, pointing an accusing finger.

"Me? What did I do?"

"This is your fault, you…you…friggin' munchkin!"

"Mom-"

"Millicent. That's enough."

"No, Mom. This is so, completely unfair," Millie continues. "Why do I have to suffer because of this It and Dull D'asia? I can never have anything I want. I forever have to hear how it's not right because my sisters can't have it too. How is that my fault, Mom? It's your problem, not mine!"

"Now, Millie, that's enough," says Laurence. "Don't talk to your mother that way."

"You are *not* my father!"

"Nor is he," Mom answers in reference to Yoan and in defense of her husband, who is way more of a dad to Millie than Yoan will ever be.

Mr. Torres shows emotion for the first time since I've been standing here. "Bernadette, I did not come here to be insulted."

"Then what exactly did you come here for? All you do is bring trouble to this house by having absolutely zero discretion in what you allow her to have. You play no role in your daughter's life, just give, give, give. Is that how you parent Gabe and Jorge? I think not."

"Mom, leave him alone. You're the one that chose him…that tried to trap him and now you're making me suffer for your poor judgment."

I want so badly to slip out the back door but it's like watching a train wreck. It's gruesome and you know you'll have nightmares but you can't look away.

Mom rushes toward the counter and stops short, slamming her palms down hard. "Is this what you've been telling her? That I trapped you?"

"I'm leaving," Mr. Torres says as he stands from the stool.

"Leave. Get out of my home. If this is the nonsense you've been feeding my child, go and don't come back. We're better off without you!"

Laurence attempts to calm my mother by rubbing her shoulders. She's fuming and her face is contorted. She looks as though she wants to cry but refuses to give Mr. Torres the satisfaction.

"Mom, stop it," Millie cries out, tears raining down her face. "Dad, please. Dad, don't go."

Millie rushes after her father, trying hard to convince him to not leave. He stops, mumbles some words that only the two of them can hear before kissing her softly on the forehead and turning to walk out of our front door.

The house is suddenly eerily silent. Mom is standing with her hands pressed against the marble countertop, her head dropped low. Laurence stands with his head back and eyes to the ceiling, his fingers digging lovingly into Mom's flesh. Millie watches from behind the screen door as her father runs away – as usual. And me? I, more than anything, wish I'd stayed where I was, in Erika's guest bed with Bette Middleton licking my cheek.

"Ma, pee-poo mad wake me up."

All eyes go to the top of the stairwell. Laurence steps away from Mom. "I'll deal with Maddex. You'll be okay?"

Mom nods. I use this distraction to attempt my great escape.

"It's all *your* fault," Millie screams rushing in my direction. "And after I was nice to you. Ugh!"

I spin around to face her. "Stop blaming me."

"I hate you. And D'asia, I hate both of you!"

"Millicent Ezan Torres-McKenna. Don't you dare *ever* say such a thing to or about your sisters, *ever* again. Do you hear me?"

"I hate this house and everything about it! I can't wait to leave. As soon as I graduate, I'm gong to Paris and never coming back!" And in the perfect dramatic ending to the perfect dramatic speech, Millie turns and rushes up the stairwell, at one point nearly losing her footing and stumbling forward. She grabs the banister and steadies herself before continuing. I so want to laugh out loud but I don't think it'll help matters, so I keep quiet.

"Millie, come back here and discuss this like a young adult. Millicent!"

Mom let's out an exasperated sigh and refrains from going after my sister, and instead picks up the mug that Mr. Torres was drinking out of and carries it to the sink. I surrender and come fully indoors. I take the seat that Millie's dad was in. So much for our budding sisterly relationship. I guess Erika and Simone were right all along.

"Guess you changed your mind about Millie getting a car for her birthday," I say softly, hoping that Millie isn't somewhere above within earshot.

Mom turns to face me, leaning against the sink again and folding her arms across her chest. "No. No, I did not change my mind."

"Then I don't understand why she's so upset." And that's when I notice it. The set of car keys left behind on the island. I lift them with my index finger and Mom nods slowly. The big H emblem says it all. "Honda?"

"Civic Hybrid. In silver, the color she wanted."

"Mom," I groan.

"It's cute."

"From a Benzo to a Civic?"

"It's a car."

I shake my head. I'm not judging my mom but it's a big switch and, though I am by no means taking Millie's side, she should've said something before now. Typical Mom but I keep my thoughts to myself. For two seconds I feel for Millie, I completely understand how she feels.

I replace the keys on the counter and stand. The moment is past. I inform my mother that I'll be going back to the Bellflower's, maybe for a few days. She thinks it's a good idea. It's a safe bet there will be no celebratory lunch today. And even better [and I use the word sooo loosely] it's going to be a very long rest of summer vacation. I can't believe I'm saying this, but I can't wait for D'asia to come home.

B-igger Cups

The first day of school is less than two weeks away. That means Demitry Haggardy's kickback is only one week away. Simone has spent the better part of the past week searching for the perfect 'fit for the night. The choices are between a short red and black skirt with knee high red and black striped socks and a black top, or a vintage red tee with a faded pic of Jimi Hendrix and jeggings with her fav knee high Chuck T's [What can I say? She loves her Chucks].

I already know what I will wear. I got this super cute purple embroidered romper from Forever 21 that I have yet to sport outside the fitting room. I think I may have subconsciously been saving it for such an occasion as this. No, I'm not too concerned about what to wear, it's getting an invite in the first place that's the trouble.

Demitry made it very clear that me and my girls are not

welcome at her party. Simone made even clearer the importance of our being there, while Erika is so completely disinterested. But she *has* to be there. We're a team. If one is the weak link, we're all losers. Therefore we've got to be at this party somehow…some way.

Operation Party Crasher

The four of us, Erika, Simone, Reilly, and me, are gathered closely around the picnic table in my backyard. It's a super hot day, like near 90 degrees, so we're drinking Mom's cherry-lemonade like it's fashion forward.

Reilly is hovered over a notebook scribbling intently. Erika has her back to us, reading the latest from Judy Blume. She thinks we're insane and just being totes ridiculous for all our plotting and scheming, and doesn't hesitate in letting us know.

"You guys are insane. This is ridiculous. Screw the stupid party. We can have our own party."

"Lame," says Simone, pouring another glass of 'ade.

"She's right, Erika. That would be pretty lame. Besides, who would come? Everyone that's anyone will be at Demitry's," I remind her.

"We don't need them. We can have our own party, just us." Erika glances at Reilly. "Just the *three* of us."

Simone and I look to each other and shake our heads. "Lame."

Erika closes the book, using her thumb as a bookmark, and turns toward us. "We don't even like her."

"So," says Simone.

"So why are we trying to impress her?"

"We're not trying to impress her, per se," I state.

"Y'all don't need to impress *her*," Reilly offers. "It ain't even about her. She ain't nobody. But in the grand scheme of things, your freshman class in general, attending this l'il shimmy-sham she throwin', it's like e'rythang."

Erika's eyes become slits. "E-ve-ry-thing! And besides, how does this even concern you? You're only going to 7th grade, what do you know?"

"Apparently more than you." Reilly rolls her eyes to the back of her head. "Look, I'm just tryna help y'all, that's it. Take it or leave it."

"I'll leave it." Erika turns back to her book.

"I'll take it," Simone says. "Reilly's right, it's not about Demitry. Well, not exactly. It's about the Wilma Rudolph freshman class."

I'm intrigued but clueless. "Yea, and?"

"So, like, everybody is gonna be in the house. That means nearly every 14 and 15 year old in Eden Grove and the surrounding area."

"Riiiight?"

"We just need to be seen there. We don't exactly need to stick and stay, just be seen."

Reilly jumps from the table and takes Simone's hand in hers, raising it in the air like she just won a championship or something. "Hecky yea, Simone. That's what I'm talkin' 'bout. That's the kinda ingenuity you need. You are a genius!"

"That's the first time she's heard that," Erika mumbles snidely.

Simone shoots her evil eyes. "You're just mad because you didn't think of it, Ms. Smarty Pants."

"That doesn't make sense, cause I could care less. As a matter of fact, count me out."

"Fine."

"Fine."

"Wait," I intervene. "Erika, you have to do this. We're a team."

"I don't have to do anything but maintain my 4.0 GPA so I can get into a good university, not spend my life trying to impress stupid pop kids that will never accept us as one of their own anyway."

"You don't even have a 4.0 GPA," Simone reminds her.

"Frontin'," Reilly mumbles.

"Not yet, but I will in high school and you're just jealous of that, both of you." Erika closes the book and sets it down hard on the picnic table. She's irritated because her grade point average is sort of a sore point with her. She's been trying her best to get a 4.0 and maintain it but she always averages 2-5 points shy. "Ali, be real with me. Why do you want to do this? I get why Suzy Social Climber does, but why do you?"

"Now who's jealous?" Simone asks. She sticks her tongue at Erika who rolls her eyes in return. Reilly laughs.

I sigh and turn to sit fully on the bench. My eyes drop to my nails and I pick nothing from beneath them. "I'm not even 5 feet tall. Millie is my sister and she's 5'6", gorgeous, and a model. D'asia is already 5' and maybe not the greatest looker on the block since she puts like, zero effort into her appearance, but she's smart. Genius. I'm just a mediocre student."

"That's because you're lazy."

"Lazy. Whatever, call it what you want. I'm a beast at soccer but most kids don't care about the sport. They like basketball and lacrosse. And the girls on the volleyball team get all the attention. Even in my own circle, Simone is hot and you're super intelligent. What do I have to offer?"

"Wait – why is she the hot one?" Erika asks.

"Need a mirror?" Simone responds.

"Uhm, can we stay focused on me?"

All falls silent. I don't think anyone really knows what to say to make me feel better. The silence doesn't really help the cause at all.

"Umm, Al," says Reilly, breaking things up. "I hate to say this but I think your life just got suckier."

My friends and I look up to see a golden skinned beauty walking in my direction. Her hair is flattened and hanging well beyond her shoulders, blowing in the breeze created from her stride. Her brown eyes look brighter in the sunshine. The peach sundress she's wearing pops against her complexion and the chunky wrist jewelry is the perfect adornment. Matching peach gladiator sandals lace up her slender calves.

"D'asia?" Simone questions.

I nod slowly, totally in awe and unsure how to react. Am I happy she's home? Do I have questions about her trip? Or am I more curious about this new look she's sporting and where it came from?

"Hey guys," my sister calls as she waves to us.

I stand and walk her way in slow motion. My arms are outstretched for a hug, which is customary when you haven't seen a loved one in quite awhile but I freeze. Suddenly I'm unable to move. As she steps closer, a broad smile on her face and her arms open to receive my embrace, I realize something more significant than any other change – she's towering over me!!

D'asia wraps her arms around me, pulling my face against her chin and says something like, it's good to be home or I'm glad to see you, or something. I have no idea because at this point, I'm totally freaking out on the inside and completely having an out of body experience. As my spirit hovers above the figures of my little sister [and I use that word loosely] and me, I come to terms with like, the worst thing that could have ever happened. D'asia is even taller than me than before and not only that but, this hug confirms my even greater suspicion.

D'asia Raquel McKenna has boobs!

"Wow. She's gorgeous," I hear Reilly say.

"Even prettier than Millie," I hear Simone say.

I could just die. Right here, right now. But I don't die [which would probably be for the best]. Instead, I faint.

Everything & Nothing

It's one of the last days to just lie around and enjoy warmth and sunshine – and the women in my family want to spend it shopping. Okay, this isn't exactly such a horrible way to spend a Saturday afternoon and normally I'd be totally psyched to engage. But no. Not when the motivation is ultimately revolved around two things:

a) D'asia's left boob and…

b) D'asia's right boob.

I lay stretched out across the grass, head to head with Justin who has been back from soccer camp in Cali for a couple weeks now. He returned a much better player than he left. His back heel has improved greatly and I'm actually kinda jealy because mine was much better before he left. He tried to teach me while running drills with some kids from the block. Teach *me*?! Ugh!

So, let's recap my summer break:

FIRST, D'asia takes away my freshman year by somehow managing to get promoted at the last possible second. THEN, she takes away my dreams by jacking me for my Vogelsinger money and uses it for her stoopid science school crap. NOW, here I am at Piedmont Park, hiding from my family because she went and grew nearly 2 inches and a whole cup size and they can't stop bragging about it!

That's the real reason why I'm here. Hiding. I had to get away. It was just too much to handle. Mom. Aunt Vee. Tee Tee Yashi. Auntie Jackie. Erika's mom, Mrs. Bellflower. Millie. D'asia. And a slew of female cousins. So I slipped out. I doubt anyone noticed. They weren't hardly paying any attention to me anyway, unless downing me to uplift D'asia is equivalent to paying me attention.

Earlier in the day...

"I can't believe little D'asia McKenna done went and got her some boobies," Aunt Vee says, astonished.

"A true Greene girl," says Tee Tee Yashi. "You know how we do."

"Robust Beauties, baby."

And in unison, "Robust Beauties!" Then laughter and lame-o, old-lady-*we're still hip* high fives.

"That's my baby," my mom says. It's like she's proud of D'asia or something; like she developed at 13 on purpose. That is not an achievement that warrants pride. It's…it's…biology. "Becoming a little woman. First she gets her period. Now she's getting curves. We're going to have to watch out for these little boys."

"You shole are, little sis. She's turning out to be a gorgeous thing. You should get her some contacts, Dette. Let her flaunt them beautiful hazel eyes."

Tee Tee Yashi: "Her eyes ain't hazel, Vee."

Aunt Vee: "Yes they are hazel. I know my colors."

Mom: "Clearly not. They're brown."

Aunt Vee: "Whatever, chile. Them glasses ain't doin' her no justice. She's a beauty and she got some pretty eyes that the world should see."

Mrs. Bellflower: "Mmhm. Just like Millie. Millie knows she's gorgeous."

Auntie Jackie: "You know she's modeling now, sis."

Aunt Vee: "Do I know she's modeling. What kinda sense that make? Of course I know my niece is modeling. You wanna do that cat run stuff, don't you?"

Does it really matter who said what at this point? Fine, I'll keep the order.

Millie laughs. "Cat walk, Aunt Vee. It's called a cat walk."

Aunt Vee: "That's in Paris?"

Tee Tee Yashi: "It's wherever she end up going, sis. It can be New York. Italy. Paris. Wherever."

Millie: "I'm going to Paris after I graduate."

Mom: "She thinks she's going to Paris."

"Mom," Millie whines.

"College," says Mom.

Auntie Jackie: "Dette, leave the girl along. Let her do her thang. You did. That's how she got here."

"Jackie!"

"Jackie what? Let the girl go model. She should. She's beautiful in that exotic sorta way. Skinny as all get out but them curves say Greene all day long!"

Tee Tee Yashi: "All the Greene girls got it going on."

Auntie Jackie: "Most. Ali must got them McKenna genes."

Tee Tee Yashi: "Squirrel, you haven't gotten your period yet, have you?"

Aunt Vee: "Naw she ain't got her period yet. Do you remember attending a Graduation Party for her? I mean, a *real* Graduation Party? She will though. I ain't in no hurry for my baby Squirrel to grow up."

Mrs. Bellflower: "She's going to high school and she hasn't gotten her womanhood yet?"

Mom: "It's the sports, girl. If the child will cut back on running around with those little boys out there, maybe her hormones will balance out and who knows what sort of progress she'll make."

Auntie Jackie: "She need to get them grades up, goin' to high school, neva mind a period. Nay say her mouth be gettin' her messed up in school. You wanna go to a good college, don't you? You better dig in them books like D'asia do."

Mom: "Oh she's getting it together this school year or there will be no soccer."

Tee Tee Yashi: "Speaking of soccer, D'asia, how was your camp?"

Speaking of soccer how was science school? Wow. And that's the point where I'd had just about enough and slipped out the back door and took off for Justin's.

Me and Justin lay in the grass, temple to temple, drenched in sweat. I just barely led my team to victory against him. Camp has done him a great deal of justice and I can only imagine what it would have done for me. Not gonna be salty. Not gonna be salty.

I hear my name being called. Least I think I do but who would know that I'm here? Not unless someone narc'd on me but who would? I'm thinking that maybe it's just my subconscious bugging me.

"Mom, I found her!"

Now that is so not my imagination. I sit up partway, leaning back on my forearms. In the distance I see a brown figure headed my way, followed by two others.

"Is that D'asia?" Justin asks, shooting up so quick that I swear he's gonna throw his back out.

I snarl and ease back onto my back, pretending that I'm completely unaware that anyone is after me. "Yeah, it's her."

"Wow. She…she's fine."

"Oh, not you too." I sit upright again. My eyes squint in the sun. She's wearing yellow shorts that I recall coming right above her knees before she left for Texas. Now they are mid thigh and I think how inappropriate of Mom to allow her young daughter to wear something so revealing. I lean forward, squinting more and trying to make out the white graphic tank. She wasn't wearing that when I left. It's not even her shirt. I recognize it too and it belongs to Millie and Millie doesn't share [remember], so what's this all about?

I jump to my feet and my hands land on my hips. "What?" I growl.

"We're ready to go shopping but we're waiting on you!"

Justin rises slowly beside me. "What happened to her? She's beautiful."

I turn sharply to face my friend. "What are you saying?"

"I'm saying that she's hot, that's what I'm saying. And I'm wondering when and how that happened?"

"What about Erika?"

"What about her? She don't like me no how."

A sound escapes my vocal chords but I can't really describe what it is. Maybe disdain. I feel my face scrunch and I charge forward. All I need is to watch my GBFF lust over my little sister. I keep walking past D'asia even as she scolds me on our mother's behalf. Erika and Millie are following and expressing their own rant at me for having shortened their shopping afternoon.

I could care less about any of this or any of them right now. I'd rather be home alone and that's exactly what I say to my mother when I get to the car.

"Ali, why? School starts in a week. You need some new shoes and clothes and I can't promise I'll have more time to take you before school begins."

"I don't care."

Mom chuckles. "Since when do you not care about shopping?"

"Mom...I just...can't I just stay home?"

"Sweetheart, what's wrong? Oh, you're not upset about that little conversation between the sisters today."

"Mom."

"What is it, Ali?"

Before I can say anything else, Millie approaches and shoves me out the way so she can get in the passenger seat. D'asia and Erika climb in the backseat, leaving the door open and middle seat vacant for me. For the first time I notice the other cars parked behind Mom. Auntie Jackie and my cousin Faye are yelling at me but I tune them out. My eyes are locked on Mom's, pleading with her to leave me behind.

"What are you waiting on, you troll? You're letting the air conditioning out," Millie grunts.

"Millicent. I'm not having it today. Alijah, get in the car. Let's go."

"But-"

"Alijah, please."

I exhale the negative energy I'm feeling and, totally against my will, join my sister and bestee in the back seat.

Wilma Rudolph

Everyone Who's Anyone

The three of us stand on the sidewalk outside of Demitry Haggardy's home. We must look like some kinda stalkers. Simone went all out. Dark mascara makes her brown eyes pop. She pinned a piece of hot pink hair in with her own which is now bone straight. She settled on a black and pink tutu with black leggings beneath and a purple cami top. Her lips are red [her mom would kill her if she saw she'd been in her makeup kit] and silver feathers hang from her ears. Not my style, but cute nonetheless.

I'm just wearing a simple jungle green romper and black thong sandals. Reilly created the cutest hairstyle for me. She made six twists that ended in a ponytail that she turned into soft ringlet curls.

Laughter to our rear jars us. Three girls that I vaguely recognize brush past us. Simone waves, a big toothy grin on her face. I fully expect the girls to snicker at her and keep on inside but one slows, causing her friends to slow down too.

"Hey, do I know you?"

"Yes. I mean, no. Well, sorta. I mean, I worked for your mom for a week over spring break."

The girl's eyes brighten with recognition. "Simone, right?"

"Yep, that's me. You're Karlie, right? Karlie Rygluski."

"Yeah. So cool to see you here, only a lame would miss this party. You coming to Wilma Rudolph next year, right?"

Simone nods dumbly. "Yeah, sure am."

"Cool. Well, why are you guys just standing around here? The fun is that way."

"We're uhm…we…"

Erika jumps in, "…are waiting for…another friend. Hear it's pretty packed inside and we want to make sure she can find us."

"Awesome. Well, guess I'll see you inside."

Simone nods and refuses to lose the goofy, toothy smile. "Yep. See you there."

The girl turns away and rejoins her friends.

"Only a lame would miss this party. Told you," Simone directs her words primarily at Erika once the girl is out of earshot. "She's a sophomore. There are sophomores here."

A group of boys charge by us, nearly toppling us over. We catch each other and stop from falling.

"Stupid boys," Erika cries out. "Why don't you watch where you're going? Whatever happened to manners?"

I rush to cover her mouth and cease her rant. The girls and the guys stare at us while they wait for someone to open the door.

Someone says something apparently humorous and they all laugh in our direction. I grab Simone by the wrist and pull both girls away to the cover of a large tree.

"You're *trying* to make us complete and total social outcasts, aren't you?" I ask Erika, through gritted teeth.

"Those boys were rude."

"News flash. All boys are rude."

Simone folds her arms across her chest. "You're wearing that stupid outfit on purpose just to spite me, I just know it. And now you're making a scene."

"What's wrong with my outfit?" Erika asks, raising her voice an octave higher than acceptable under the circumstances.

I resist the urge to scold her tone and instead deal with the issue that Simone addressed. "Nothing if it was laundry day."

"Oh, I hate you two." Erika turns to stalk away.

I look to Simone who has an expression that reads, *let her go*. I jog after Erika. "Erika, wait. Please. Look, I know you don't care about this stuff but me and Simone do. Why can't you just do it for us?"

"Duh. Ali, in case you didn't notice this, I'm here."

"You're not. Not really. You couldn't even bother to pull a decent outfit together and don't forget, I know you have clothes. I was there when your mom bought 'em."

Erika shoots her eyes to the heavens and crosses her arms in front of her. She taps her Birkenstocked foot against the concrete. Her jeans are rolled up to give them the feel of capris. The t-shirt she's wearing reads Arthur Ashe Community Picnic '88 and it's a size too big. I have no idea who its original owner was but clearly it isn't her. She's wearing her glasses [that she like, never wears] and her hair is in a bun. Aaaand we're supposed to believe that this isn't intentional. Hmpf.

"If I'm such an embarrassment, why don't I just go home and you and Simone do this without me."

"Because we're a team," says Simone. "And we don't bail on each other. You're coming. We're either gonna rise or fall but whatever we do, we're doing it together."

I'm impressed. "That was deep."

Simone snarls at me. "I'm smart."

"I didn't say you weren't."

"Yeah, whatev. Anyhow, here's what we're gonna do…"

Simone and me pull Erika behind a tree and proceed to make her look as decent as possible. Simone unrolls the jeans and turns the oversized tee into a midriff. The sight of belly button can improve any outfit. She takes the bun out and pulls it into an alligator braid instead. We look over our work and nod approval. Not fly, but at least acceptable.

"So now what?" I ask.

"D'asia," Simone says.

"What about her? What's she got to do with anything?"

"It *is* D'asia," Erika says, astounded.

PAUSE. Did she just say it *is* D'asia, as in D'asia *is* here? I turn in time to see my little sister approaching with Justin and a few others from our graduating class. Needless to say I'm a little more than angry, that would put it mildly. First off, Justin refused to go on this mission with us – and I mean REFUSED – because he claimed to have some sick duty as an invited guest to not aid and abet party crashers. Labels, have we learned nothing? Said it would hurt his image and in high school image is everything [duh, that's why we want in]. So where is he going with my little sister, because she is soooo certainly NOT invited!

I charge from the cover of the tree without thinking.

Justin looks startled as he well should. "Ali."

"Justin. What are you doing? You totally blew me off and you bring a 7th grader?"

"Technically, Ali-" D'asia begins.

"Technically I'm not speaking to you. Does Mom even know you're here?"

"As a matter of fact she does."

"And she's okay with Justin taking you on a date to a wild party."

"Ali-" Justin interrupts.

"Shh. Now I'm not talking to you. D'asia?"

And do you know she has the audacity to roll her eyes at me?! "It's not a date. It's Justin. He's like our brother. And yes, Mom said I can go. She thinks it'll be great to meet some kids that I'll be going to school with next year. And well, if you're at the party, how wild can it possibly be?"

Was that a burn? I shrug it off.

"Number one, Justin has been checking for you, which makes this a date. And more important, do you know who's party this is? Demitry Haggardy," I answer before she can say anything, "and she doesn't let anyone in without an invite."

"So I suppose that means you guys won't be getting in."

I gasp. Because I can't say anything, only gasp. Since when is my little sister so snarky?

"She has an invite, Ali," Justin informs me.

"She has a what?" My ears must be broken or something because I could not have heard Justin correctly.

Simone pushes in front of me. "You were invited?"

"Yeah. I saw Demitry when I went with Millie to pick up dinner the other night and she asked if I wanted to come. Millie said I should go. Said it would be good for me going into Wilma Rudolph as an advanced student, and all. Get me in good with the pop kids so I won't have any trouble."

Now, I'm seething. This just gets better and better. When is Millie concerned about either of our well-being? I just don't get it.

"She invited you," I state more than ask.

"Yes, she invited me."

"Did you stop and ask yourself why? You know she only did it to score final hour cool points with Millie and to spite me."

"So what. Who cares?"

"You should."

"But I don't."

"This is awesome," Simone squeals and I clench my fists tight so I don't slap her. "We'll just go with D'asia. I mean, she's your sister so Demitry can't turn you away, and me and Erika are with you so it's like, some kinda effect."

"Domino."

"What does pizza have to do with it?"

I close my eyes and grind my teeth. This can't be happening... this can't be happening...this can't be happening... I listen to Erika's voice as she suggests that this is a good thing actually. How I wanted in and something about Simone's Social Ladder Etiquette has sound reasoning. She can turn me away with Justin but not with D'asia if she is indeed an invited guest.

"No, no, no," I cry out.

"Ali, don't be ridiculous," Simone says. "This is our opportunity."

"No."

"You're being a child."

"News flash, Simone, I *am* a child."

"That doesn't mean you get to act like one."

"Hey, Ali."

I turn to see who said my name and when I do, my breath catches. The voice belongs to exactly who I thought it did – Gage Campbell.

"H-hey," I answer nervously. *Don't blow it, McKenna.*

He smiles, showing those perfect white teeth. What was I angry about again? "Glad you made it. Didn't think Demi would've invited you. Glad to see she's maturing. You guys coming inside, or what? I mean, she *did* invite you right?"

I look to Erika who looks to Simone who looks at me. "Uhm. Yeah. Of...course. Like we'd show up to a party uninvited. How lame would that be?" I chuckle nervously.

"Looks like you got your perfect in after all," Justin grumbles with an eyeroll, to which I respond with a *shut-your-stupid-face* death stare.

Gage nods, seemingly unconvinced, but invites us to follow him and Jeremy Leiding onto Demitry's property. We wait on the porch, my girls and me holding one collective breath while waiting for the door to open. Demitry's mouth completely drops when she sees us there with Gage and Jeremy. I'd laugh if I wasn't so nervous.

She can barely form a coherent sentence. "Gage, what...Ali you're not invited," she finally spits out through gritted teeth. "Why are you here?"

I look, in utter embarrassment, to Gage who steps back like a gentleman and let's us go first. "Don't be silly, Demi. It's a party. The more the merrier. And to think, I just gave you credit for being so mature, like a real highschooler. Thought you were ready for an adult relationship. Guess I was wrong."

"What? No, I mean, yes...I mean...I'm mature."

Gage only shakes his head in disappointment and keeps past.

Demitry struggles to speak but all she can seem to utter is an internal squeal. I know I have zero boobs but I swear in this moment I do and they sit up just that much higher as I pass the threshold into Demitry Haggardy's evil lair. Just for the moment I forget about D'asia's soaring popularity and Justin's betrayal. I put aside the look of disappointment that Gage left me with and every other negativity in my life at present. I'm not Millie's sister and the brunt of every short joke known to Eden Grove. All that is going to matter is that we were here and in the eyes of those that are clueless as to how we came to be in attendance on this evening, we're cool and therefore acceptable, and that is all that matters. I guess life can improve. ☺

Spoke 2 Soon

High School.

It can make a person or completely ruin their existence. And I do mean completely. Have you ever seen a talk show? Any talk show. Oprah. Wendy. Maury. Jerry. Who cares. Someone always has some crazy low self-esteem issue that leads to other ridiculous life choices like:

a. drug addiction

b. alcoholism

c. prostitution

d. any other sort of dependency or co-dependency you can think of.

I would so like to think that I'm stronger than those people and that my future doesn't call for me being a guest on whatever the latest and greatest talk show will be at that time, talking about how I never amounted to anything in life and do unthinkable, unspeakable acts to make a living to support me and my 7 rugrats because Demitry Haggardy made my life miserable in the 9th grade.

That's a major part of why attending that kickback was so crucial. Simone was right about the importance of being in the house, even though Erika thought it was all a croc. Even Millie made D'asia go. Why? Because she totally knew the importance of establishing oneself before entering high school, especially as an underage AP geek. There were very specific rules of engagement in place...rules that Millicent E. Torres-McKenna was the underwriter for. And if she was pushing D'asia, I knew in that moment that we had to be there.

Thank goodness for Gage Campbell.

Sigh…Gage. The look on Demitry's face when he guided me and my friends in was priceless. Okay, so that was the end of our engagement. I'd hoped he'd dance with me or get me a drink or something. He totally igged me once inside, but at least we were being ignored *inside*. And Demitry's evening completely unraveled from that point on, so in the end it was all worth it. Even if she's now making me pay and immediately undoing any good being seen at her party may have done.

"Watch out, shrimp!"

It felt like it was happening in slow motion. And not the romantic fantasy kind like the first time Gage approached Simone, Erika, and me at graduation. No. This is way more twisted and horrid. I'm staring down a speeding volleyball and it's going to take my head off and there is nothing I can do about it.

Now for this to make any sense, I gotta take you back in time to about a half hour ago…

Physical Education 101

"I hate gym. It's so for the birds," Simone says, adjusting the altered uniform top and smacking her glossy peach lips together. It's always something with her. This school year she's actually cut the short sleeves down the middle and tied them back together.

"You're lazy."

"Says the pot."

"Nice try but not the same."

"Whatev. Am not. I just don't like to sweat, too cute for all that. Oh my goodness, Ali. It's like 3rd period. I kinda don't want to go all day smelling like…like…gymnasium sweat."

I laugh at first, but then stop abruptly. "OMG. OMG. OMG."

"What is – ahhh. He's got PE with us?"

"Uhm, duh. He's in uniform."

"A little weird, right? He's a sophomore."

"So is half our PE class, Simone." Gage Campbell steps onto the court looking like a vision. He daps Jeremy, smiling and showing off a slight dimple. He glances my way and he so does a double take when he sees me. He gives me a head nod and my stomach turns all kinds of knots.

"He's checking you out," Simone says through tight lips.

"Is not."

"Totally is."

"Well, maybe a little," I concede. I wiggle my fingers in his direction, like the cool girls do in cool kid movies. Cute. Kinda coy. Then my arm drops abruptly and my smile fades. Demitry and Kamahla are standing right behind him, scowling at me. "You think she saw."

"Yeah. So."

"So? So, I'm not trying to tick her off more than I already have. It's the first day of school. So far so good and I don't need her ruining things for me."

Simone shrugs and adjusts the clip she's using to keep the back of her shirt bunched and above her belly button.

"Alright, you pansies, time to get down and dirty," Mr. Aguirre cries out. So he separates us into two teams for a good old-fashioned game of volleyball. I'm with Gage [hooray!] and Demitry [groan...]. Simone and Kamahla are with the opposition.

"Any volunteers to serve?" Mr. Aguirre asks in his gruff, *I've-smoked-cigs-since-2nd-grade* voice. "No? Fine. We'll go with you and uhmm…you."

I point at my chest and he confirms.

"Are you any good at volleyball, grass fairy?" Demitry asks.

My eyes turn to slits but I suppress the urge to say what I really feel. I can't start the school year out in the principal's office. Mom would literally kill me.

"I'm good at every sport."

"Yea, well, you better be."

I close my eyes and count to 3 as I head to my position. I set and serve and Haille Brennon spikes it for our first of many points. Game on. I'm in the zone and Gage notices and sidles up beside me. Demitry is up to serve.

"You're really good at this," Gage says to me.

I smile. "Thanks. I'm like thee biggest sports fan, ever."

"You think you're gonna play for the Panthers this year?"

"Hoping for varsity." My fingers are crossed when I answer. Not trying to jinx it.

"Varsity? That's a big goal for a freshie."

"Yeah, and? I hear you started on the varsity lacrosse team *and* football team last year."

Gage Campbell blushes – and it's soooo cute! "Yea, well-"

And that's when it happens –

"Watch out, shrimp," Demitry yells.

When I look over, it's too late. She's too close, the serve too powerful, and the warning intentionally too delayed! One minute I'm making small talk with Gage [and I was actually talking, not just imagining it!] and the next…darkness.

"Oh my gosh, Ali-Cat. You okay?" Erika rushes to my side in the nurse's office.

"Yeah, yeah," I grumble, struggling to sit up without dropping the bag of ice I'm holding to my eye.

"How did this happen?"

"Phy Ed. Competitive sports, and I'm not talking about the game of volleyball we were playing. How'd you even find out I was here."

"Avery Hightower said Jada Carlton said Viv Blanks told her that Mary Michele said that Demitry and Kamahla jumped you in the locker room after gym. That's not true, is it? Where was Simone when all of this was going down?"

"Wow, how do these rumors get started?" I swing my legs over the side of the tiny bed. It can't be a twin size. If I were 10 lbs heavier I wouldn't fit. I wonder how normal people fit on it without tipping over. "Didn't quite happen that way but yeah, Demitry's responsible nonetheless."

"So, what do you plan to do?" She takes my forearm in her hand and guides me forward like I broke my leg rather than blacked my eye.

And that's the burning question. I can't fight her. Not on the first day of school. Besides, this is high school and I don't want a reputation as some sort of thug. I have a future career in the pros to think about. But she can't just get away with it. But she pretty much just did. I'm so sure she batted her eyes at Mr. Aguirre and claimed it was an accident and he fell for it. Pretty little liar. How perfect.

I sigh in exasperation. "Go to my next class, I guess."

"That's it?"

"What can I do about it? She'll just say it was an accident and they'll believe her without question, you know it. If I lash out, I'll look like a fool and that's what she wants."

Erika beams like a proud mom. Yeah, so I'm taking the high road on this one. This time. But I do so hope there isn't a next time.

D'asia With A Flower

High School. The final frontier. Okay, maybe that's a little dramatic but I've only been in this place for a couple weeks now and it's already sucking so bad. This is so not the plan. This isn't how it was supposed to be. I already spent the better part of my educational life being…well, not at the bottom of the barrel but not far from it, despite having a sister who was the reigning queen. But she was the evil half sister – and I was her Cinderella.

But even Cinderella had her day and her prince. When and where is mine?

Every day during the 11 o'clock hour I am forced to deal with Demitry Haggardy and her accomplice, Kamahla Choudhary. And if I even breathe too hard in Gage's direction, alarms sound and all out war is declared against me and Simone [who's only guilty of having the wrong friend at the wrong time]. And no differently than classes shared at Arthur Ashe, it would seem the Superintendent's daughter continues to have teachers wrapped around her privileged little finger.

I never cared about her one way or another but I'm beginning to really haaa....disliiiike – no, loathe her. Loathe: to feel disgust or intense aversion for. Yes. That perfectly describes my feelings for Demitry Haggardy.

And if Millie was zero help to me in grammar school, she's absolutely not helpful now. The Honda Civic grudge. That's what she's holding against me. Oh my gosh, like it's my fault that Mom changed her mind about the Benzo. In all honesty, I don't think mom was ever down with it to begin with and I'm going to tell you why [and it has nothing to do with D'asia and me]: Mom doesn't drive a Benz, so how do you process having a kid that drives a car that costs like $40, 000 more than yours??

Doesn't take a rocket scientist – or a D'asia McKenna even – to figure that one out.

But still, she hardly speaks to me at home and if she sees me in the hall at school, she snubs me. I guess it's better than her actually saying something to me that ends in shrimp, imp, git [as in midget], elfkin, dwarf, smurf, or any other *clever* insult she can come up with in the spur of the moment. I guess in that regard she respects the biological connection, which is fascinating in and of itself. She must *really* be mad.

But where biology is concerned, stranger things have happened. Just think about the things we learn about the inner workings of the human body. Mitosis for example. Like, how is it that the cells even know that they should split? But they do because so much is depending on them doing their job.

Even more fascinating than mitosis and...well, I'm not the science geek, D'asia is, but even more fascinating than thee most fascinating scientifical fact that you can think of, is Millie and D'asia's transition from consequential enemies to nearly best friends. That is correct, Millie and D'asia are now actual friends, despite the fact that per Millie Logic both D'asia and me are equally responsible for her life of rolling a Honda Civic. Talk about unfair! It all started when D'asia came back from Texas taller, prettier, and with curves that were non-existent when she left. Now, you can't keep those two apart. It's like Millie has her own pet now, or something.

Exhibit A Flowing Hair

"Wow, D'asia. Look how pretty your hair is. I didn't realize it was so long. You should let me flat iron it like Aunt Bev did when you were in Texas. Here, use my clip."

We all have long hair – when it's pressed and combed. Who's surprised that D'asia actually has a decent length of it? Millie obviously. She's such a dingbat.

Exhibit B: Hour Glass

"Oh my friggin' gosh, D! Look, your girls are growing in so nicely. They are so perky, I'm jealous. And look at you getting hips and bum! Here, wear my shirt."

PAUSE. Uhm, since when are we allowed to call D'asia, D?? Or is it only her new best friend that has the honor of calling her that?

Exhibit C: ANTM

"Wow, D'asia, you're almost a normal height! If you grow like 3 more inches, I'll totally hook you up with Claude Dubois, my agent. Maybe you can do some modeling too. You're so pretty, just like me."

Here, take my sucky personality.

Grrrr.... See what I mean? Fascinating.

Normally when Mom, Laurence, and Maddie come through the door it sounds something like: *Girls, I'm home!* And whoever's around at the time drops what they're doing and comes down to greet her. She asks us how our day went, we ask about hers, she inquires if we're hungry, we of course are, someone takes charge of Maddex and gets him settled in [usually this person is me], then Mom heads to the kitchen and assigns responsibilities and we help her prepare dinner. Simple enough. Pleasant enough.

But sometimes the greeting is a little bit different.

"Alijah McKenna!"

No one that lives in my home with me is home with me. It's just me, Erika, and Simone in my room studying when my mother bellows. Simone's eyes go to Erika and Erika to Simone's before all four land on me. I know what they're thinking: What did Ali do now?

But I didn't do anything this time. Okay, I was late for first period...and second but that was absolutely not my fault. Millie is ultimately to blame and it's so completely unfair.

I try to control my eye rolling as I drop my pencil on the desk beside my Algebra book and rise from the chair. I don't know why, but I feel like I'm walking the green mile. I've gotten in trouble plenty but it's so much worse when it's so unjust. Mom hates getting calls from school, she doesn't care what it's about. If a representative of the Eden Grove School District is calling her at work, you'd better be dead or dying.

I pause knowingly at the top of the stairwell. Knowing what it's about and knowing how this really ticks her off. "Yes?"

"Don't talk to me from up there. You know how that ticks me off."

I descend slowly, ill-prepared to be scolded. The day was already so sucky. First, I oversleep. I'm gonna miss the bus, no doubt about it. So, I ask Millie if she can give me a ride. She tells me she can't because she already agreed to give D'asia one and according to her, she asked first. As for me, there's no room because Laura and Lauren expect to be picked up and it's too short notice to change plans now.

Never mind that the advantage of my being small is I can fit in nearly anywhere and she never mentioned picking up a 3rd party so there is room in the back. But I don't address this, clearly she's still holding this ridiculous grudge which is somehow solely my fault and D'asia is off scot-free. I won't beg Millie for anything. Instead, I turn on my heels and go back to my bedroom and pull up Google on my laptop and find the site for EGTA [Eden Grove Transit Authority] and figure the fastest route to Wilma Rudolph.

Since I miss the connecting bus, I miss the entire first period and I'm so late for second period that I get sent directly to detention. Great. This means my first class of the day is PE and now I'm wishing that I would have somehow missed that one too. Demitry makes class difficult as usual by finding some sneaky way to totally humiliate me, with Mr. Aguirre being none the wiser [or pretending to not notice].

And if things couldn't get any worse, sixth period takes the cake. If Gage Campbell is the cutest boy ever, Jordan Price is a close second. So I'm standing outside of Ms. Beasley's American History class waiting for the bell and chatting with Simone and

Marja Patel and up walks Justin and Jordan. Justin wraps an arm around my neck and pulls me to him, saying in my ear: "Hey, Ali-Cat, my boy has something he wants to ask you about and I wasn't sure how to answer."

There are like, millions of butterflies in my belly as I turn around. Jordan Price wants to ask me a question. Sweet. I'm totally psyched and I shoo Marja and Simone away. I'm preparing the answer in my mind as he approaches and opens his mouth to speak. Should I say: *Sure, I'll go out with you.* That might be too casual. How about this: *Yes, Jordan. I'd love to go out with you.* Nah, too desperate. Okay, got it: *Cool, whatev.* Yeah. That's it. Makes me totally mysterious.

"...so what do you think?"

I missed the question! "Wh-what was that?"

"D'asia, she's your sister, right?"

"Yyyeeesss..."

"So you think she'll go out with me?"

I bite down on the inside of my mouth so hard that I nearly pluck away flesh. "She's thirteen," I say with zero emotion.

He's unimpressed. "So. I'm fourteen. She's a freshie, right? We're in the same grade. She's so hot. Yeah, I think I'm gonna ask her out. Thanks."

And he pats my shoulder as he rushes inside the class at the bell like...like...like I'm the homie or a stray cat or something. I'm so dumbfounded that I'm frozen in place and don't move until I realize that Ms. Beasley has just closed and locked the classroom door!

I rush forward and tap on the glass but she just points down the hall and returns to the days lesson. Two detentions in one day.

Can things get any worse?

"I had a long day, so I'm not prepared to debate this. You're grounded for the rest of the week. Now take Maddie and give him his bath. And tell Erika and Simone to go home, you'll see them tomorrow. Where are your sisters?"

"Wait. What?" I guess it can.

"You heard me."

"But don't you even care what happened? I asked Millie to drive me to school cause I accidentally overslept and she claimed there was no room but that was a lie and she took D'asia, so why shouldn't she take me too? We're all going to the same place. And now she's not even home and she didn't call to check in or ask permission-"

Mom sighs heavily and puts her fingers to her temples and I stop speaking. Laurence steps in and tells me that he'll deal with Maddex and asks that I not give my mom a hard time because she had a hard day. I really want to say that I did too but I only nod.

"Millie should have taken you but it's your responsibility to get up on time. But Ali, that has nothing to do with you skipping sixth period."

"But I didn't-"

"I don't wanna hear it. This is high school. Grow up. Life is about more than whatever ball you're playing with; soccer ball, basketball, baseball, I'm unconcerned. My hours were cut with Vance Dewitt and now I need to take on a second job to help Laurence keep up with the expenses around here until he can get back to work full time again. Honestly, I don't have the energy to follow behind you and make sure you're doing your job properly."

I'm dumbstruck. None of it is fair. Not at all. But what am I to say now? Mom works so hard as it is and to have to take a second job because her husband got laid off of his great paying job and had to take part time gigs and now her hours are cut? Well it sucks. It does but that doesn't make it okay to take it out on me either.

Mom continues, "As for D'asia, I spoke to her earlier and gave her permission to stay after with Millie for cheerleading tryouts. I only thought they'd be home by now. But what I need you to do right now is…"

Mom's voice fades to somewhere in the background. My eyes nearly bulge out of my head. I turn at the sound of my friends creeping down the steps. *Cheerleading tryouts!* I mouth the words. I can't even tell them bye or gauge their reaction as I pass them on my way up the stairwell. I pause when I arrive at the top landing and notice it for the first time. The sign matching the one hanging on Millie's bedroom door that reads: Property of D'asia

Since when does she spell her name with a flower?!!

D'asia

☉ Chicken Out ☉

They are like best friends now. When did this happen?" I pop a dry chicken nugget in my mouth and chew with a frown on my face. It sucks that Erika is in AP classes cause we hardly ever see each other during the school day. Fortunately we both got 5th period lunch. The only thing that could've made it better is if Simone had it too but she got stuck with 6th.

Erika makes a strange face that I read as her trying to hide something from me. And I've known her for like, ever, so I know when she's being shady.

"What is it?" I ask.

"What's what?" Erika asks, playing dumb. She adjusts her glasses on her nose even though they don't need adjustment.

"That face. What is it?" I wait, and when she still doesn't answer, I push. "What are you hide – you're friends with her!"

She rolls her eyes to the top of her head and shrugs it off but

I'm so unconvinced. Something is totally going on and Erika's trying to hide it from me.

"We're not friends."

"You're something with her. You guys have a bunch of classes together so now you're replacing me with my annoying little sister?"

"No one is replacing you, Ali-Cat. Don't be such a drama queen."

"Oh. Em. Gee."

Erika exhales heavily and drops a nibbled on nugget in a pool of ketchup. "She's not so bad. That's all I'm saying."

"She's not so bad. She's not so bad? She doesn't even speak. She's like…she's like…the queen of geeky mutes and suddenly everyone wants to be her best friend. She's not even supposed to be here. Why isn't she at Arthur Ashe? I had to do a full eight grade school years, why shouldn't she?"

I lean back in my seat, fuming. I don't believe this. Nerds are supposed to get picked on…teased. I should be defending her. But she's single-handedly ruining my life.

"She's smart – really smart. I'm smart but she's…she's like a savant or something. But at the same time, she's a pretty cool person."

I groan for lack of anything remotely intelligent to say. It's all just really rather annoying.

"What do you want from me?" Erika asks.

"I don't know, loyalty maybe."

"Oh my goodness, Ali. I mean, really. She's your sister."

"She's a mute."

Erika's eyes divert behind her black frames and a new expression falls across her face.

"Oh, what now?"

"Not anymore. She speaks. And she's funny. She like, has a whole personality that she just kept to herself."

"She grows boobs and gets a press out and now everyone wants to be her bf."

I sigh and slump forward. I snatch a cold fry from Erika's tray and stab it in her ketchup, pushing the stray nugget aside. My eyes scan the lunchroom. Everywhere I look people look pleased. Like their lives are perfection. I glance at the door and freeze. I forget to breathe on time and cough to catch my breath.

"What?" Erika follows my line of sight.

Gage Campbell and Sidney Black enter with another guy and two girls, neither of which are Demitry Haggardy. I feel Erika's irritation. I think she likes Gage less now than ever before. He laughs, showing those gorgeous teeth. He glances up and his eyes meet mine and I swear I'm going to melt and slip down the nearest drain. He nods at me and I smile so hard my cheeks hurt.

What do I do? Should I go over to him? Should I say something? I fidget a bit before I decide that saying hello is the right thing to do in this situation. I swallow hard and open my mouth to speak but it's too late, he turns his attention to the curly haired girl to his left. He says something to her and nods toward me. She laughs.

"Ali," Erika says with force. I jerk to attention. "Don't go there."

"What?"

She rolls her eyes and picks up her tray as she stands from the table.

"What?" I ask again.

"Just please don't be stupid."

"What. Ev."

"Yeah, whatev."

Boy Trouble

I never thought I'd see the day. Never. Not in a million years. Not in a hundred million years, even if we all somehow survived Zombie Apocalypse, did I ever think it would be possible to see it. D'asia Raquel McKenna [now officially D, or D'asia with a flower if she's spelling it out] is hot and becoming popular.

When did this happen? At some point over summer break in Texas, while living it up with science and sunshine. It started there and blossomed beneath Millie's tutelage.

How did this happen? Good luck and good genes that managed to miss me in my mother's womb.

Why did this happen? To add to the catastrophe that is my existence, why else?

I stand at the door speechless, staring into the eyes of Jordan Price. Yes, the same Jordan Price that Justin gave me the impression wanted to ask *me* out. Okay, well, so what he didn't say anything at all to imply such a thing but what else was I to think? I surely never assumed he would want to know anything about my little pain in the rear.

And now, here he is, escorted by Justin who already pushed past me and entered my domain. For a moment I ponder whether or not he has anything in common with a vampire. Can I rescind his invite and make him fly involuntarily out of my crib? And I'm just about to try when he walks behind me and pushes me aside.

"Ali, don't be rude. C'mon, J."

I step back as Jordan crosses the threshold. Like I said before, he's no Gage Campbell, but he's pretty nonetheless. He's brown with dimpled cheeks and a really nice smile. His hair is cut low and he's conservative in an olive polo shirt, brown shorts that come just past his knees, and hi top Michael Jordan sneakers. His kicks would be totally fitting if he played basketball too but he's on the football team.

"This handsome young man must be Jordan," I hear my mother say.

I walk out the front door and take a seat on the stoop. I don't need to hear anymore. I can't believe my mother is allowing her thirteen-year-old to go on a date with a high school boy. It's… it's unconscionable. That's what it is, purely unconscionable. We have no idea what this boys intentions are with our D'asia and furthermore, she's too sheltered to date so soon.

Fine. Referring to this as a date may not be exactly how my mother and Laurence see it. There's a new Seth Rogan movie out and me, Erika, Simone, Justin, Jordan, and D'asia are going. Technically it's friends spending a Friday night on the town having innocent fun except I know how Jordan and D'asia are really looking at this scenario. This is just a clever little way for them to spend some time together.

"Alijah!"

I jerk to attention and see Reilly standing at the bottom of the steps. When did she get here? "Hey. When did you get here?"

"Dang, girl. Wassup wit' you? You out of it."

I shake my head. "Nothing. I'm fine. Just waiting on Erika and Simone to get here."

"Oh yeah, y'all going to the movies. I forgot."

"Yeah…wish you could go. You sure your mom won't change her mind?"

Reilly trots up the steps and takes a seat beside me. She folds her arms across her knees and rests her chin there. "Seth is my dude, too. But nah. Ma Dukes be trippin', straight up, yo. She say I'm too grown for my own good as it is. I don't need to be seeing no PG13 movies without adult supervision. Plus she think I'm too young to be hangin' with a buncha high school peeps."

"Oh."

"Yeah. I mean, I tried to explain that it's purely a technicality but she ain't hear me though."

We look up at the sound of voices headed in our direction. It's Erika and Simone. Simone opens the gate and skips through, climbing the steps and taking a seat after greeting Reilly and me. Erika, on the other hand, enters super apprehensively.

"You're going too?" She asks Reilly.

Reilly rolls her eyes and stands. "I like you, Ali. And I like *you*, Simone."

"I like you, too," Simone responds.

"But your girl, she need to learn some manners. I can teach her if y'all want."

Erika's expression goes from one of disbelief to irritation. "Who are you talking to, little girl?"

"Definitely not you," she answers in that raspy tone that I've come to adore, and I can't help but chuckle. "No worries, E. I'm not going. I just came by to speak to Ali. She's my friend too, y'know."

"Well maybe you need to get some friends your own age."

Reilly just smiles. "Hey, maybe you're right. Guess if I took yours, there'd be no one left who would tolerate you. I'm not a selfish person. You need them more than I do. See you later Al's... Simone."

"Ugh, I can't stand that girl!"

"Let it go," I say as I wave goodbye before returning to my state of self-pity and aggravation. I hug my knees and let my chin sink deep between. Simone leans against me, resting her head on the outside of my thigh.

"So Mom is ready to take us to the theater if you guys are ready," says Erika, but I don't respond. "What's with you?"

"You'll see in a sec."

And as though on cue, the voices inside my house make their way to the front door and out steps Justin and Jordan. Greetings go around and Erika and Simone eye-speak and I signal for them to just wait for it. Moments later the door opens once more and out steps D'asia.

Mom has flat ironed her hair and curled the ends. She wears contacts now since Auntie Jackie thought that her new fly look was being hindered by the bulky eyeglass frames she wore previously. Her face is freshly scrubbed since Millie got her started exfoliating and – wait, I hadn't noticed before but it looks like Millie even arched her eyebrows! Just great. She's wearing a hot pink v-neck top and deep blue denim, and a pair of small gold hoops that Aunt Bev bought her while she was away. They sent me a pair too but I don't wear them out of spite.

An elbow belonging to Simone keeps jabbing me in my side and it's so annoying me. "What?" I say through gritted teeth.

"She's getting prettier every time."

"Yeah, thanks Simone. That's totally helpful."

"What? I'm just saying."

"Yeah, well I'd prefer if you didn't." I roll my eyes and turn away, jogging down the steps and leading the way to Erika's house.

Simone catches up to me. "Y'know, you would be just as pretty if you stopped trying to be such a tomboy and put a little effort into your look. You know I'd totes help with that...please let me help."

Frenemy says what?!

I move my legs faster, separating myself from Simone before I say something that I can't take back.

"Ali-Cat! What's wrong? Was it something I said?"

I'm so glad the movie is over. I couldn't even enjoy it. Not with all the giggling and flirting going on between D'asia and Jordan. I'm just ready to go home but it seems like everyone else wants to hang out. It's late...like 9. We should go home but I'm outvoted. Simone wants ice cream from Bill & Ames and Justin agrees. Says he hasn't had a vanilla bean and sweet potato sundae in two whole weeks.

For a sec I swear that Erika is totally on my team because she votes against Bill & Ames. Then I realize that she's hungry for more than ice cream and would rather go to Duncan's for cheese fries. Jordan and D'asia are all googly eyes and hardly notice that the rest of us even exist. I stand to the side, fuming. Discreetly of course. Everyone doesn't need to know that I'm jealous. Kind of jealous.

Not completely, just a bit.

"Why are you so jealy?" Justin says in my ear, scaring the crap out of me. I nearly jump out of my skin and my arms fall to my sides. I turn toward him and slap him hard on the chest.

"I'm not jealy. Why would I be jealy? Jealous of what? D'asia and some stupid boy? News flash, Jordan Price is not the only boy in Eden Grove, y'know."

"True, but besides Gage, he's the only boy you care about."

I speak firmly and through gritted teeth, "I don't care about Jordan or Gage or any other stupid boy in Eden Grove, including *you*. Ugh."

I stalk past him toward Erika and Simone but not before hearing him grumble the word *jealous* one last time.

I stand, shifting back and forth while Simone and Erika debate which locale is the most sensible one. My eyes lock on Jordan and D'asia. I don't mean for them to. It's like, they have a mind of their own or something. They're standing close – too close. She's all gazing up into his bistre brown eyes [yay, art class] and he's touching the ends of her hair. I feel my lids lower into a squint. Then she does that silly thing I've seen Millie do on countless occasions. She giggles and taps him gently on the arm. Like he said something so funny. Doubtful. Clearly this is a reflection of another coveted Millie's Outlook on Life lesson.

"Ali."

I stumble to the side and hurry to catch my balance so I don't tip over. I turn an evil gaze to Erika.

"You pushed me."

"Pay attention."

"Why did you push me?"

"Because I was calling your name for like, ever and you're so deep into D's biz that you can't even hear."

"D? Did you just call her, D?" Did she just call her D?

"Oh. Em. Gee," Simone says as she steps in front of me. She firmly wraps both of her massive hands around my small biceps. "Can you be less obvious, please. It's kinda sad, Ali-Cat."

"What are you talking about?"

She leans closer and her voice is a whisper when she speaks. "Your jealousy."

"My what?" My voice is not so subtle. "Can't we just go home? I have stuff to do."

"What stuff?" Simone questions doubtfully.

"Stuff. Homework stuff."

"You have what?" Erika can barely get the question out before she's laughing so hard I think she's gonna pop a vein. "Did you say…did she just say…homework stuff? Oh, *now* I have heard it all."

"You're lame."

"And you, my dear, are a – dare I say it, Simone?"

"Say it, girl. It's for her own good."

"You are a hater."

My eyes widen in disbelief. *I* am not a hater. Just because I don't want my little sister dating some high school…stud, does not make me a hater. And that is precisely what I tell my friends [or so called, cause they're not being very friendly right now].

"Hater," Simone sings.

I try to find a proper response but only stammer.

Justin walks up behind me again, but this time I'm aware. "Who's a hater?"

"Ali-Cat."

"Am not," I growl. I shove past them. So judgmental, I can't stand it. Leave them bickering about whether or not I'm a jealous hater and if we should go to one end of downtown for Bill & Ames when Duncan's sells ice cream almost as good [though none flavored with sweet potato which is surprisingly delicious].

I don't need them, I don't need any of them. I have money and a bus will be headed this way in about 15 minutes. They can have cheese ice cream for all I care, but I'm going home. I take three steps and –

"Ah, look who's here. Hey, how come no one told me the circus was in town? I love to see the little people perform their balancing act."

The small group surrounding Demitry chuckles at her joke. Why me? This night can't get any worse.

"Hey, Ali." Gage steps forward and wraps his arm lazily around Demitry's neck.

Clearly I was wrong. I'm always wrong. I swallow hard but say nothing. My eyes go from Gage to Demitry and back. Oh, why won't my lips move?!

"She's short *and* deaf," Demitry jokes viciously. "Must suck. Honey, maybe you should sign it so she'll understand. Wait guys, maybe she can't see us this high up. She doesn't know who we are."

This is the moment that I fall in love with Gage Campbell. He gives her a disgusted look and takes his arm back, shaking his head. "You shouldn't call me honey. I told you, we're not back together. Not until you can stop acting like a little kid." I watch as he rolls his eyes and shakes his head and steps away but not before saying to me. "Cute shirt."

"Honey – I mean, Gagey!" Demitry whines.

I look down like I totally forgot what I was wearing. Actually, in the moment I really do forget. I glance at my hot pink and gray tunic and smile appreciatively at myself. I look up quickly to say thanks, but as usual I'm too late. He's gone but Demitry Haggardy is still here, with her little cronies at her side. I guess someone from my group finally notices what's going on because they all rush to my aid. Not that I need them to, but I'm glad that they do so nonetheless. That's what friends are for.

"You think you're so cute, don't you, McKenna?"

With Gage out the picture I get to feel confident again. "I don't have to. Your boyfriend thinks it for me. Oh wait, that's right. You're not back together, are you?"

She lets out a strange noise. Sorta like a squeal and a growl that come out simultaneously. "Look, he didn't say *you* were cute, he said your shirt was. And it must be way too dark out here for him or maybe he needs glasses because that pink is pukerific. Idiot."

"Idiot?" Simone and Erika repeat at the same time.

"Yeah, idiot," Kamahla and Mya reply.

D'asia adds, "Looks like your boyfriend or your not-your-boyfriend, whatever, I'm confused as are you, is checkin' for another girl while he's out with you. That has to be worth at least 10 points in my book. Is my math right, Justin?"

"I think she's right, Demi. And y'know, she's a genius and all, so I wouldn't question her calculations."

"So if I carry the one, who's the bigger idiot now?"

We all turn to see Gage standing a few yards away, looping a finger through the end of a curl attached to the head of the girl I saw him with in the cafeteria a few days ago. My stomach sinks and I think I'm going to dissolve into the earth below but feel better when we all look back to Demitry whose brown face is now beet red and eyes are slits. She makes that weird sound again and stalks away.

"You okay, sis?" D'asia asks.

I smile slowly. Maybe…I was wrong. Maybe D'asia – or D, isn't so bad after all. "I'm fine. Thanks, sis."

"Anytime."

"That was awesome," says Jordan, closing the gap between the two of them yet again. "You're beautiful, smart, and sassy. You're incredible."

Eh, maybe I spoke too soon.

Eva Longoria

🫦 New Attitude

I stand stock still…frozen in place in front of my mom's closet. I don't think I'm even breathing. I mean, I must be because I'm somehow not dead but I don't feel myself breathing. I think I should put my hand to my chest to make sure it's rising and falling but I can't move. See, if do anything logical in this moment it most certainly means acknowledging what it is I'm about to do and the steps that I have taken up to this point. And if I do that, I just may totally freak. I need to go forward with my plan. It's the only possible way of me having a somewhat decent life in high school.

"Here goes," I mumble and take a delicate, bare toe step forward into mom's walk-in closet. I'm in it now. And now that I am here, there really is no turning back.

Here is how it all began:

"Ali. Ali." That's D'asia, standing in my doorway and whispering my name. I hear her, of course. I'm just ignoring her. "Ali, I know you hear me."

I close the People Magazine that I took from my mom's pile in the basket by the toilet, and turn to face her. I say nothing, just stare. This is how it's been between us for the past couple weeks. Ever since I found out that she was spending time after school between cheerleading practice with Gage Campbell. MY GAGE CAMPBELL!

"C'mon, Als, don't be like this."

"Don't call me Als and I won't call you D. What do you want?"

"You can call me D, I don't mind."

"I don't wanna call you D! Since when do *you* wanna be called – ugh, what do you want?"

"May I come in?"

"Why Gage?"

"Sorry. I didn't know you liked him."

"Not true, everyone knows." I return my attention to the magazine.

"Fine, I knew. I'm sorry. But we're just friends. I mean, he asked me out the other day but – " When I give her the most evil look I can summon she quickly gets to the point. "Look, Ali, I need a favor."

"From me? Why don't you ask your best bud, Millicent? She seems to have taken you under her corrupt wing," I answer with dripping sarcasm.

"Well *you* sure didn't."

I close the magazine again and turn on the bed to face her. "And what's that supposed to mean?"

She sighs heavily. "Nothing. Look, you're my big sis too and I need a huge favor from you."

Now I sigh heavily. I nod sharply, signaling for her to come in. She does and closes the door gently behind her. "Jordan wants to officially take me on a date."

I groan and turn over onto my stomach. "So."

"So, mom is not going to let me go if she knows it's a date. Like, an actual date."

"Let me guess –"

"I need you to come with…and then disappear."

"What happened to my guess?"

"Just for a little while. Like, a couple hours. Long enough for us to see a movie and get some ice cream from Bill & Ames."

"Hmm, let me think about it for a sec. No."

"Why not?"

"Just no."

"Come on. This is the sort of thing that normal sisters do for each other."

"News flash, D'asia. We are not normal sisters."

"But we could be."

I say nothing even though I feel myself starting to get weak. The bed shifts as she stands and I listen as she slowly walks toward my door.

I exhale most of my irritation with her. We are sisters and I guess this is something a sister should do. "Fine."

"You'll go?"

"If, and only if Erika, Simone, or both can go with."

"Then you'll go?"

"Yeah, sure. Whatever."

Then she squealed. Like a trapped rat, she squeals and rushes from my room to get ready for her 1st official date *and* rebellious act. I exhale as much hate as I possibly can before reaching for the phone.

Well, Simone went with and we saw a movie in a different theater and had burgers at Gillingham's next door to Bill & Ames and not-so-little D'asia got to have her very first date – before me. How fair is that? When I got home the *People* that I'd been reading earlier that day was on my bed and in it was a feature article on Eva Longoria. I mean, she's super hot and all the guys love her and she's only 5'2" and hardly 100 lbs.

KEY WORDS in that statement: Super. Hot.

So, fast-forward back to this moment in time and here I am in my mom's closet looking for a pair of heels to wear with my Easter dress from last year [yeah, so what. It's not like you can tell it's an Easter dress]. I pretended to leave for the school bus this morning, and once D'asia left with Millie for school I came out of hiding and broke into Millie's makeup stash. I think I did a good job on my face.

I'm clueless about what to do with my hair so I just brushed it back into a ponytail. I put a little of Millie's mango butter on the edges to make sure it's neat. I sprayed on Mom's Donna Karan just the way I've seen her do it. Both wrists, neck, behind the ears, balls of my feet. I was just about to put it back exactly where I found it but stopped short. I considered for a moment, then sprayed it in the air and danced beneath it just to be sure people will be able to smell me.

Now, I only need a pair of heels to complete the look and it's off to the city bus and hopefully I'll get to school in time for 2nd hour. The school will call to report my truancy from 1st hour but I'll deal with that when the time comes. I take a deep breath and grab a cute pair of 4" red heels with a flowery bow on the toe and rush from inside as though I'm scared alarms will sound. A size and a half too big, but nothing a pair of small socks stuffed inside won't take care of.

I look at my reflection in the full-length mirror on the back of the door. The dress is teal polyester with a sheer overlay, with straps and a satin ribbon that ties in the back. A little formal for school but I don't have many options in my closet filled with jeans and t-shirts. My cheeks are super rosey red but it *is* called blush, right? I take a deep breath and glance at the clock. If I'm gonna make it in time I gotta go now.

I look around and make sure everything but the shoes I'm wearing is in place, then rush from my mom's bedroom and down the stairs, struggling to find balance along the way. Wow, I'm pretty high up. But it'll be worth it to get Gage's attention. So long as I don't run into Millie or D'asia [which I rarely ever do], everything should be just fine. I grab my book bag and make sure the auto lock is engaged, and rush out the front door.

"What are you wearing and why are you wearing it? And where were you 1st hour?" Simone asks when I run into her near our lockers.

Before I can reply, up walks Justin with Jordan Price at his side. He sneers. "What in the world are you wearing?"

"Clothes," I reply sarcastically.

"You look silly," he says, and keeps walking past.

"Do not," I yell after him.

Simone leans close to my ear. "Is that your Easter dress from last year?"

I roll my eyes. "Yes. Yes, it is."

"Why are you wearing it? It's so totally passé."

"What does that even mean? Do you know?"

"Old. Past tense. And…wait. Are those Mrs. Carter's Valentino shoes? Do you have a death wish?"

I must. "Let's just go before the bell."

I stumble away trying my very best to keep my footing en route to Algebra I. I tune out the sound of Simone snickering on her way to her US History class.

I walk from the toilet stalls barefoot across this grimy locker room floor toward the locker where I stored mom's expensive shoes and the rest of my stuff. Gym so completely sucked today. My feet are already killing me and I spazed on my need for sneakers this morning and Mr. Stupid PE Teacher refused to accept my reason for wanting to skip class participation on the grounds that I had unacceptable footwear. Told me that was what I get for treating 3rd hour like it was prom night and if I didn't participate I wouldn't get credit. I can live with that. What I couldn't live with was the inevitable phone call home. One call to intercept is enough. So I participate in bare feet.

Of course stupid Demitry Haggardy had the time of her life trying to take my head off every time during, of all things, a game of DODGE BALL! Somehow I managed not to fall over to the credit of lots and lots of years of athleticism.

I just want this day to be done. So far my plan isn't working at all. Justin and Simone both laughed at me, not to mention the series of snickering that's become the soundtrack to my day. I made a fool of myself in Phy Ed in front of Gage and gave Demitry something else to make fun of me about. And now, as I sit on the bench waiting for Simone to finish her shower, rubbing my aching feet [and it's only 3rd hour!], I have to suffer through the sound of Demitry on the other side of the lockers cracking jokes and cackling, no doubt at my expense.

Sigh. I reach over and move my ridiculous dress aside to get to my undergarments. I slip on my pink underwear with the word FRIDAY written across them, grateful that today is actually Friday. I pause as I almost get them to my waist. I glance down and my heart stops. I finish pulling them up and tighten my scratchy re-used white towel. I'm panicking…I'm panicking. I pick up my dress and accidentally toss it in the air.

"Hey," Simone cries out from beneath it.

"Where is it?" I mumble. I drop to my knees kinda hard, but ignore the pain. I feel around under the bench. "Where is it?"

"Where's what?" Simone asks, tossing the dress back at me.

"Looking for this?"

PAUSE because I can't breathe. I hear Demitry behind me and I'm pretty sure she has what I can't find and now I just can't breathe. I listen to the sounds of footsteps gathering.

"Looking for this?" Demitry asks in her snotty, I'm-better-than-everyone voice.

"Toilet tissue?" Simone asks sounding totally dumbfounded.

I wanna cry. I really wanna cry but I won't give her the satisfaction. I turn around in slow motion. When I crawl from beneath the bench and look up, I see Demitry hovering with a stupid grin on her face. Nearly every girl from class is around her. Kamahla's arms are behind her back and she looks super satisfied while Simone, who is standing between us, just looks baffled.

"Some girls got it, and some girls don't. You're so stupid if you think my Gagey won't know the difference between Charmin and real…tissue." Fyi, that pause was so that she could squeeze her own boobs. She's stuffing too, I just know it. No way she grew two whole cup sizes since the start of the school year.

My cheeks are so hot, I swear steam must be coming from them. Simone mouths the words, *You stuffed?* and I give her evil eyes. Like now is really the time to judge me.

Demitry rubs my fake boobs between her fingers before continuing. "Guys, it's not even Charmin. It's single-ply!"

And the crowd goes wild. Kamahla moves her arm forward and reveals my itty bitty training bra that she's been holding by the tips of her fingers like it's contaminated or something. Demitry and Kamahla both drop my belongings to the floor and turn to walk away but not before warning me to: *Stay away from Gage Campbell!*

I drop my head toward the floor. I'm humiliated. Totally and utterly humiliated. I stand upright and Simone rushes to my aide.

"Oh, Ali-Cat."

I raise my hand sharply, warning her not to speak.

"But why would –"

I raise my hand once again, hoping she gets it this time.

"Ali, what's going –"

"Shh," and I, again, raise my hand.

She opens her mouth and I watch her contemplate saying something to me, and she watches me contemplate taking my anger out on her if she does. I pick up my useless bra from the floor and get dressed side by Simone's side in silence. I know she's struggling not to speak to me and ask questions that I'm not ready to answer. I can literally feel it.

I rush from the locker room stumbling and limping along as the first bell sounds. Simone rushes after me, calling my name but I pretend not to hear her. I try to hurry down the steps. Since she has a class on this level, maybe she won't follow but I'm wrong and I can't move all that fast thanks to my choice of attire. Stupid Eva Longoria.

"Alijah, please. Just wait up. I just wanna knows what's going on," Simone calls.

"I said, shhhh."

"Hey, Ali!" I glance up and see Demitry, Mya, Kamahla, and a couple others leaning over the rail and looking down at me. Mya blinks a few times and does a super dramatic, super entertaining display before finally pretending to sneeze. "Got a Kleenex?"

The girls from gym class roar with laughter. I wanna run but I can't. Instead I try to walk faster but somehow I miss the step that I was aiming for and land hard on the one after it. So hard that the heel snaps, sending my ankle sideways. The rest is a blur. I reach out to grab the banister but it's not enough and my body is thrown down several really hard stairs before I finally stop myself three steps from the bottom.

I don't need to tune out the sound of laughter. A blanket of shame that covers me quiets everything else when I struggle to get to my feet, only to find that I am face to face with *gulp* Gage Campbell! I want to run. My brain screams, FLIGHT! But my stupid achy feet and painful twisted ankle won't let me. Seems he came down after me when I fell.

I see his lips moving but I can hear nothing. I only stare. Like the idiot that Demitry Haggardy accused me of being, I stand with all my weight on one leg, and just stare. His lips move again but still, no sound. He reaches out and I watch his hand move slowly toward me and I subconsciously stop breathing. He's almost touching me when I feel a pair of hands on my upper arms ushering me away.

I'm conscious once again. The sounds of laughter confirm it.

"Is she okay?" Gage asks Simone.

"She'll be fine," she lies for me as she guides me to safety.

"Gage Campbell thinks I'm an idiot," I say through a thick pool of tears stuck in my throat.

"I think you're an idiot," Simone says, and I nod in agreement.

♡ R.I.P.

Hmmm…. I'm thinking. How do I want my tombstone to read?

Here lies Alijah Dominique McKenna. Mediocre student. Questionable sister and horrible daughter who broke her mother's only pair of Valentino shoes and thus…her heart.

That sounds about right.

I step awkwardly from the school bus wearing a pair of well-worn borrowed New Balance sneakers that are two sizes too big. They belong to Erika. After my tumble of shame, Simone guided me, limping to Erika's class and managed to get permission for her to leave temporarily so she could lend me her shoes. It was either that, I go barefoot, or borrow Simone's whose feet are already a size 10.5.

Once we got the shoes, Simone escorted me to the school nurse to get ice to ease the pain and swelling in my twisted ankle. It wasn't broken and she said I'd likely be okay but she'd have to call my mom and tell her what happened. Oh joy. Mom, of course, wanted to rush up to the school to get me and I would have loved for her to let me start my weekend early. But I couldn't have her come and find me in my Sunday best with her expensive heel in one hand, and the shoe it should've been attached to in the other.

Instead, I convinced her that I would be fine and that I wanted to stay. I needed to buy time to try to fix the heel, a task I figure Google is best suited for. I'm like, so relieved to be off the bus. Tuning out giggles, snickers, and snide comments said just loud enough that I can hear, is really tiring.

I feel exhausted. Like I've been playing soccer for a full game and three OT's. What's worse is I feel so totally ridiculous in my Easter dress and Erika's gym shoes, a ratty ponytail and running mascara. Worse still, I put on too much of mom's perfume and now I reek. I even flared up Ms. Waterbrook's allergies. Who knew?

I finger wave to Simone and Erika. I say nothing. I have nothing to say. Erika asks if I want them to come over after they check in. I shake my head. Simone asks if I'm sure. I wave her off and limp slowly toward home, sighing in relief when I confirm that Millie and D'asia aren't home yet but at cheerleading practice.

I climb the steps of the front porch and drop my heavy bag in front of the door. I kneel and unzip it so I can get my keys. My keys…my keys… Where are my keys? My poor little heart starts racing again. If it keeps being jarred like this it's bound to attack me. I unzip another pocket, then another. Nothing. I turn the bag upside down and dump the contents, heels and all. I don't have my keys. Where could they – ?

I think back to this morning. I looked in the mirror. Rushed downstairs. Grabbed my bag. Checked the lock – and left my house keys on the end table. No, no, no, no, no! Mom and Maddex and Laurence will be home in like an hour and a half and I need to be cleaned and changed with a repaired pair of Valentino heels back in mom's closet and an incriminating message mysteriously deleted from voicemail.

I shoot upright. "Crap. Crap. Crap. What do I do, what do I do?"

I have an idea and rush as quickly as I can, without stepping down on my bad ankle, around to the back of the house and try the back door. It's locked as expected. But there is a window above the kitchen sink that's never locked. It's a bit of a struggle to get to it with a twisted ankle.

There's a low back porch just three steps from the ground. If I climb on the ledge and stretch from my tip toes to finger tips, I can just reach the window ledge. All I need is to get a grip and pull myself up. Once there, I just brace myself against the wall for support, press my hands firmly against the window and…and… why isn't the window going up?

I take a breath and brace myself once again, place my hands firmly against the glass once again and…nothing! Nothing happens.

That means…it's locked! Someone locked it? What idiot would lock the window *above the sink*? Like someone would go through the trouble of breaking in through that window. Ridiculous.

It can't be locked. This is the best way to break into my house and of all days, someone decided to be safety conscious?! I swear. I feel myself panicking. I have to get inside. I'm running out of time. How could this happen? This can't be. I try again and again to push the window up, pressing harder and harder to no avail. In irrational frustration I slap my open palms hard against the window and command it to open.

"Let me in! Let me in! Ah!"

I've lost my balance. I just lay here. In my Easter dress, on my back in the grass beneath the locked window that was once a security breach. My ankle throbbing. I can feel a tear trail the side of my face. It makes me itch but I have *no energy* to scratch it.

"Ali?"

I jerk to attention. I glance around and notice I'm still outside and it's getting dark. I wonder what I'm doing here. But when I look down and catch of glimpse of teal, all the events of the day come flooding back. I look up into the faces of Mom, Laurence, and Maddex.

"Awi, why you seep outside, Awi? You got bed in your woom."

My smile at my little brother is much kinder than I feel.

"Yes, why are you sleeping outside? And what are you wearing? My goodness, child, you look a mess," says Mom. She continues up the steps and toward the front door, reluctant to take her eyes off of me. Laurence helps me to my feet and I mumble a thanks.

I hear the sound of Millie's Honda pulling up and I rush past Mom as soon as she pushes the door open, and head up the stairs to my room. Mom's gonna check the messages soon. She's going to find out that I missed first hour and call me down. I can't let Millie and D'asia see me like this.

I rip the dress off and kick one of Erika's shoes across the room, slamming it into the wall and it lands in the wastebasket by my door. Two points. The other, I remove a little gentler and toss it. I snatch my drawer open and grab a pair of shorts and a plain t-shirt, then rush into the hall and to the bathroom to scrub my face clean. I can hear Millie bragging about how much of a natural D'asia is as I limp back to my room to figure something out…anything that I can do to solve this little shoe drama. Geez.

I land hard on my bed and pick up my backpack and unzip it. I pull the shoes from inside. I drop the good shoe to floor and just kinda stare at the bad shoe while I'm holding the heel in my hand. This sucks. I mean, royally sucks. All I wanted was for the dumb kids in my freshman class to see that I can be just as hot as my stupid big sister and my even stupider little sis. I should've never let Simone get to me. Instead, I just made a fool of myself and a mess of everything – including my year old Easter dress [and mom *is* gonna, like, totally spaz out if she ever sees the big dirt and grass stain on the back that likely won't come out, not to mention the rip on the side, both courtesy of my burglary attempt [[#fail]].

Gorilla Glue. I never used it before but I remember Laurence saying how it works wonders or something, and I'm pretty sure there's some of it in the basement in his tool box.

"Alijah!"

The voice is muffled but it's undoubtedly my mom's. She must have listened to the voicemail. I take a deep breath and pray – no, beg Jesus to do me a solid and step in and save my tail just this once. I hope he hears me like I hear an angry Bernadette Carter call my name again, first, middle, et al.

I stand and trudge toward the door, being careful not to put any weight on my hurt ankle. Dead man limping. The beginning of the end. I turn the knob slowly, carefully, and step into the hall. I know what's what but I play dumb anyhow. It doesn't matter. She's been a mom for a long time. I'm sure she totally expects it.

"Y-yes?" I call from the top of the stairwell.

"Alijah Dominique, you get down here right this instance."

Okay God, just in case your son was busy and didn't hear me, please just help me out with this one. My day so sucked. Believe me, I totally learned my lesson.

I take the steps with caution, trying to smear any guilt from my face. All eyes are on me as I descend and I just wanna run and hide. The least she could have done was send Millie and D'asia to their rooms. She doesn't have to humiliate me in front of them of all people.

"Ma'am?"

"Don't ma'am me. And don't act like you don't know what this is about. Where were you during first hour, Ali?"

"I…was late."

"Late? How is that possible? I woke you up myself this morning."

She did. She cut my slumber short and made me cook turkey patties for Maddie while she took an extra long shower. "I know but…well, I…"

"And you," Mom says, turning to face Millie. "You have a car for a reason. If your sister missed her bus, why didn't you take her to school?"

"I didn't know she missed her bus," she answers in all honesty.

"How is that possible? This house is not that big."

I'm trying so hard to fix my mouth to say something helpful, but I'm kinda struggling. Right now I really wish I was a genius like D'asia.

"Well, I – "

But Millie catches my eye and cuts me off. "What I mean to say, Mom, is that...uhm, me and D left early. We had a...morning practice. Yeah, so, we were gone before the bus and that's why I didn't know."

Okay, uhm...what?? Is Millie somehow trying to help me? I mean, her explanation really only helps her but she's slow and I think *she* thinks she's being helpful.

Mom contemplates for a second. "I still don't understand how you missed the bus if I got you up this morning?"

"That was my fault," D'asia jumps in before I can speak.

"Your fault," Mom repeats.

"Yes. She was really tired and after she got dressed and stuff she told me she was going to lay down and asked if I would wake her before Millie and I left. I forgot."

Really, what is going on here? D'asia looks to me and raises her eyebrow ever so subtly. Mom doesn't catch it but I do. I turn to my mother smiling and nod. "Yeah, Mom. That's what happened."

"You girls wouldn't be lying to cover for Ali, now would you?"

Millie makes a disgusted noise and walks toward the kitchen. "Yeah Mom, did you see pigs flying on your way home from work? Or shall I say, little munchkin men."

Mom looks from Millie to D'asia, and then to me. I just shrug, so terrified of my voice betraying me and screwing this, whatever this is, up. "Laurence?"

His response is a shrug of his own. Mom sighs and mumbles the word, *whatever*. I quickly make my way to the steps, relieved, though not for long.

"But Alijah," Mom continues, "what I don't understand is the strange message from Mr. Aguirre, asking that I make sure that you don't come to gym with heels on again or he won't give you credit whether you participate or not."

Oh God, why hath thou forsaken me? I swallow hard and try to find the strength to turn around, hopefully prepared with a logical answer since I don't own a pair of heels.

"What heels was he referring to and is that how you hurt your ankle? You don't own any heels. You wanna tell me something?"

"They're mine...Mom. Mine," Millie lies – again.

"Yours."

"Yeah. I let her borrow a pair – an old pair, of course."

"And why would you do that? Ali's a tomboy. What would you possibly need with heels, and why would you wear them to gym? Okay, what is going on around here?"

"Well she – "

"No, I don't want you to tell me. Ali?"

I turn slowly on the step and face my mom. Lying to her is like the hardest thing ever. It's like she can see through your soul and know that you're trying to play her. So, I don't lie.

"I just wanted to be pretty...for once. Like Millie and D'asia." It isn't hard to say this because it isn't a lie.

Mom looks completely baffled. "Pretty? Like Mil – oh, Ali. You're beautiful."

"Mom, please. You're supposed to say that. It's like a cheap shot against you if you were to think I was a troll like the rest of the free world."

"Alijah Dominique McKenna, you are not a troll. You are gorgeous just like Millicent and just like D'asia. Don't ever allow anyone to make you feel different, do you understand?"

My eyes drop to my feet. I don't mean for them to...but that kinda raw honesty made me feel worse than I thought it would. "Yes, ma'am. Can I go to my room now?"

"Awi, pwetty," Maddex says.

"Yes, Maddie-honey. She is. Very pretty."

I watch my mother consider, hoping her encouraging words got through to me. Besides that, I'm supposed to help in the kitchen but she sighs heavily and waves me on. I turn and limp upstairs to my room, closing the door behind me. I don't cry or anything silly like that. I just sit on my window ledge and look at the neighborhood below. I'm kinda startled when my door opens, and surprised to see Millie and D'asia walk through.

No one says anything for the longest time. D'asia takes a seat on my bed and Millie stands with her back to the wall looking at me.

"Come to collect?" I ask, totally sarcastic. They wouldn't help me for no reason. D'asia maybe but never Millie. She hates me too much.

"I heard about what happened today," Millie says.

"Oh." I look away. Reilly comes into view below. She's playing kickball with some neighborhood boys. "So you come to gloat?"

"What's up with you? Why'd you wear that stupid dress and what shoes did you wear?"

I nod toward the bed. I guess D'asia caught my drift and shared my shame with my big sis because soon I hear Millie gasp and say, "Mom's Valentino's? Oh my gosh, Ali. What were you thinking?"

"I wasn't…okay. I wasn't."

"Do you have any idea how much these shoes are worth?"

"No, I don't. A lot, I guess... I just wanted –"

"To fit in, yeah I heard. But this was like thee dumbest thing ever. Mom will totally freak if she sees this."

"I know."

"This is a really expensive brand. I don't even want to say how much they probably cost and they were her anniversary gift from Laurence."

"I know."

"Really Ali, this was really stupid."

"I know."

"I thought you were much better than this."

"Well, I'm not." I turn and look her in the eyes. "You gonna tell her?"

"Of course not. Look, whatever, I don't like you and you don't like me but we're still sisters. Just…how are we gonna fix this before she notices that something is wrong?"

We??? I'm too stumped by the word "we" to mention the Gorilla Glue option.

"Laurence has some Gorilla Glue," D'asia says, stealing my thunder. She protected me. I guess I can let her have it.

"Oh my gosh, you're a genius," I say as if I would have never come up with the option on my own.

D'asia shrugs nonchalantly. "You think it'll work?"

Now Millie shrugs. "I dunno. But it has to. I don't think we have too many other options."

And like that, we're sisters. Normal, everyday sisters who protect one another. And it feels like a really great end to a totally sucky day – even though we know that it won't last. Thanks, God. Good lookin' out.

Volley Girls

very month my entire family gets together for dinner at a relative's house. Last month it was Auntie Jackie's. This month it's Tee Tee Yashi. Idk why we bother to do it here. Her house is too small for all of us. Good thing she has a huge backyard and it's still warm, else we'd be lapping up and sharing plates.

"Alijah, get your little greedy behind out my kitchen." That's not Tee Tee Yashi. It's Aunt Vee. Whatever kitchen she's in she claims is hers. I guess cause she does like 90% of the cooking, she can stake ownership over someone else's property. Funny. And what's funnier is she doesn't even have to cook all that much. Almost all the women in the fam can cook, even most of us kids. I think it makes her feel important…like she's still in charge.

"C'mon, just one more," I say, reaching for another of her famous coconut truffles. I already had three.

"No."

"Please."

"Ali, no."

"But they're soooo good, Auntie. You can't get mad at me. It's not my fault you're the best cook in the family." That part is almost true. I, personally, think Auntie Nay is better but no one would dare say this to Aunt Vee's face.

This totally gets her and she blushes. "One more, chile. Then get yo' itty bitty bizness out of here while I'm trying to get this meal done."

"Yes, ma'am," I respond, smiling and popping another truffle, savoring it's deliciousness.

I do a doorway dance with Uncle Parker. He calls me Squirrel and reminds me that I'm smaller than everyone, just in case I forgot or tried to convince myself otherwise. I wanna roll my eyes to let him know how I feel. I mean, I really wanna roll 'em to the waaay back. But knowing me, I'd get caught. Somehow, someway. Uncle Park wouldn't tell, he'd probably just laugh it off but one of my aunts would happen behind him just in time to pop me between my brows and tell me that my eyes are gonna get stuck like that and then tell my mom how disrespectful I can be and how they know she raised me better.

They so stress me out.

The house is crazy packed. I almost trip over my little cousin, Ivan and bump right into Talisa. I didn't even see her. I say I'm sorry and she somehow takes this as her cue to make a scene. She belts out a good wail that like, so does not match the little bump I gave her, and runs into her big sister Nija's arms [somehow this is pronounced Nie-ya. I don't know how or what Auntie Nay was thinking].

"What did you do?" Nija yells at me.

"I didn't see her."

"How could you not? You're almost the same height."

Really? Really, dude? Did she like, just insult me over an accident? I can't think of a clever comeback right now so I, instead, squint my eyes to let her see that I'm annoyed, then walk toward the front door.

I just need to get out of here. There's no one for me. Either the cousins are too little, too old, or too stupid for my taste. Nija's a perfect example. We should be friends, according to my mom and Nija's mom, just cause we're only a year apart [she's a year older] and maybe we could be if she wasn't like, a complete and total jerk.

You should understand something about my little town of Eden Grove. Everyone either goes to school and/or has a job. Everyone lives in a house. Some are bigger than others, but we all have basements and most of us even have our own bedroom. I think the only person in town that's even seen poverty firsthand is Reilly since she comes from Chicago. Oh, and Patty Bitters from Quinoa Road. Her family moved here from Brooklyn, New York. They have an accent and everything.

But even though in our town 87% of the kids are from a two-parent home [according to our last census] and our median income is like $93K, there is a small group of kids that are huge fans of 106 & Park and any film featuring Snoop Dogg, and think because they know every lyric to every song on the latest Lil Wayne and Wiz Khalifa CD and have seen Soul Plane like eight trillion times, that they're down with the hood and are self-proclaimed Getto Supastahs [that's literally what they call themselves. I know, right?!].

Nija's entire personality is stolen from music videos. From the weave, to the labels on her clothes, to the secret tattoo that her mom and dad absolutely do not know about, to the way she talks. She is such a poser and I wouldn't be caught dead outside of a family function with her and I'm so sure she feels the same about me.

I'm almost at the front door when I feel a tug on my jacket. When I glance over it's my mom standing there holding a worn out Maddex in her arms and a look of warning on her face.

"Where do you think you're going?"

"Just…to get some air."

She twists her lips to the side. "You can see Simone and Erika anytime. Today is about family, you know that."

"I wasn't going to go see Simone and or Erika."

"No Reilly either."

"Mom, I just need some air. It's stuffy in here."

"Then go out back. I'm watching you."

"Why are you watching me when Millie and D'asia aren't even here?" I immediately regret my flippant remark and brace myself.

Mom glares at me for thirty seconds too long and I'm on edge. "D'asia is downstairs with Tamika and Millie will be here when her father drops her off. Now, not that I owe you any explanation about how I parent, if you would like some air you can get it from the backyard while you're helping Uncle Willie on the grill. Understood?"

"Yes, ma'am," I grumble with relief for having not had my butt handed to me. I do an about face and follow Mom toward the back door.

"Awi, pwetty," Maddie mumbles, then falls into a sudden sleep in Mom's arms.

My mom disappears into Tee Tee Yashi's bedroom and I head to the basement in hopes of more excitement than what's above. A TV is playing, competing with the sound of Karmin coming from stereo speakers beside it. A couple older cousins are at a table playing Spades. D'asia and Tamika are side by side on the sofa, noses buried in their laptops. Both genius geeks. I'm so outta place. I turn and head back to the top of the steps.

"Ow."

The door stops abruptly at the expense of someone on the other side.

"I'm sorry," I say, peering around and being very careful to watch what I do before trying to open the door again. I'm face to chest with someone I don't immediately recognize. I look up into twinkling green eyes and my own eyes continue to take in the softly textured cornrows that go past his shoulder. I guess I'm staring 'cause he waves a hand in front of my face. He's cute but I'm leery 'cause this is, like, a family function. Is this a cousin that I've never met?

"Hello?" I hear a voice coming from behind him. I look around to see Millie standing there looking at me like she's completely disgusted.

I fix my mouth to say something to her but I stop. I look from her and back to the green-eyed cutie pie. Then it hits me. Oh gosh. This must be one of her little brothers. I'm so completely embarrassed. The stupid brother doesn't move and I try to squeeze out the door and pass by as quick as I can.

"Were you checking out my brother?" Millie asks, somewhere

between disgust and comedic hysteria, on the verge of doubling over in laughter.

"No," I say with lots of venom. As much as I can muster. "Eww. Why would I check out your brother?"

"You were checking him out, weren't you? I saw you, you little tree gnome."

"Oh, screw you!" I say it without thinking. I didn't mean to but my goodness! Why does she have to humiliate me like this? I mean, after all, he's *her* brother, not mine. And he's cute. Really cute. I mean like Gage Campbell cute [but cuter]. And since when does she hang out with her brothers anyhow? He could have been a friend of any number of male cousins for all I knew.

"Did you just swear at me?" She sounds like she's so astonished. But I've heard her swear, she just doesn't know it and I never tricked on her. But of course – "Mom! Mom, friggin' Mini-Me swore at me!"

I groan and look for an escape. I really don't need this right now.

"Hey," the cutie – I mean, Millie's brother, says to me.

I smile involuntarily. The goofy kind that makes it obvious that you think someone's cute. I don't have to see it, I can feel it. "Hi."

"I'm Gabe. You're the sister that plays soccer right?"

Light suddenly enters my world. I smile even goofier. "Yep. I'm that sister."

"I love soccer. I brought my ball if you wanna get out of here and kick it around with me 'til my dad comes back."

"Sure. That would be…that would be fun."

"Cool. Y'know, you're kinda cute. Is that weird to say cause your sister is my sister?"

I just shrug and make the I-dunno-sound. He asked me to kick the ball around but we don't move, we're just staring. My brown eyes locking with his asparagus green ones. Then I hear Millie's screechy and annoying voice pleading her case to my mom. I grab Gabe by the wrist and we make a beeline for the front door. Touching his skin makes my heart skip and I think that finally, Millie has done something quite nice for me, even if she hadn't meant to!

⊕ Asparagus ⊕

So, I'm sitting on the bench and waiting for Simone to finish fixing her hair. I don't think I have ever gotten dressed after PE this fast. But I needed time to fantasize about Gabe because I talked to him last night and his voice sounds so nice on the phone. He's a year younger than I am but it's okay because he's like, totally mature for an 8th grader. I think it's because he goes to that private prep school in West Eden Grove. We have talked every weekend since the family dinner. Millie doesn't know. She'd have a stroke if she ever found out.

She's such a lame, his sister and mine. She didn't even want to bring him to Tee Tee Yashi's that day. I guess Yoan is trying to prove my mom wrong about...well, everything! So he picked up Millie to take her shopping while he was taking Gabe and Jorge. Even though she came home with like, EVERYTHING, she swore that her dad wouldn't get her anything but let the boys get whatever they wanted.

Actually it was Gabe's idea to come hang with the family. He just wants to get to know Millie better and have some kinda relationship before it's too late. I don't know why, he's not missing anything. But like I said, he's so complete and totally mature for his age. And even better, he doesn't make fun of me for my size either. He thinks I'm cute. Like a doll. And he calls me that. Baby Doll. *blush*

"Oh my gosh, Aliiiiiiiiiii!"

I jump and turn to face Simone who is hovering with her hands on her hips. "Oh my gosh, what?"

"I have been calling your name forever. You're always doing this, you never listen." She gasps. "Eew, eew, eew!"

"What? Oh my gosh, what?"

She leans in close before she speaks. "You're thinking about him aren't you?"

I stand and grab my books from my locker. "Am not."

"Are too! What's his name again? Gage?"

"Gabe," I say in a low voice, slamming the locker. Gabe and Gage are too close and I don't want anyone in here to get confused and think that I'm thinking about Gage Campbell. I mean…well, I would be. And I probably will be later but right now I'm not.

"He's Millie's brother, don't you think that's just a little bit creepy?"

I stop and turn my back to the door to push out. "He's Millie's brother, Simone. Millie's."

"Creeeepy." She sings it. Like it's the hook for some stupid Katy Perry song.

"Look, I happen to like Gabe and I think he likes me. And it's not creepy or wrong," I say as I step outside the locker room, bumping into someone along the way. Am I becoming some sorta klutz, or what? I watch humor enter Simone's big, round eyes. When I turn around, lo and behold, the wicked witch of Eden Grove is standing in front of me. No, not Millie, the other one.

"You're creepy and you'd better stay away from him," Demitry cries out.

Yes, Demitry Haggardy is totally in my grill and for no reason. I don't even know what she's talking about.

"Stay away from who?"

"You know who, you...you...cretin! Gage, that's who."

"What are you talking about? I haven't even been around Gage."

"I heard you, you tree stump."

Kamahla cackles and my eyes squint. "Wow, and how long did it take you to come up with that one? You must feel really smart 'cause, like, a tree stump is short and I'm short. Whoa. Clever."

"What-ever. He doesn't like you. Just cause he said something nice to you once doesn't make you special. He's just that type of guy."

I shoot a confused glance at Simone who says two words that clear up everything. "Millie's brother."

Idiot. "Wait, I wasn't talking about Gage – "

"No need to lie," says Kamahla. "We heard what you said."

"You misunderstood. I was actually talking about –"

Demitry steps closer, cutting me off. "You just stay away from my boyfriend, okay. You don't want to mess with me. I will destroy you. You think you were embarrassed when you made a fool of yourself in those silly red pumps that day, I'll humiliate you every time you cross Gagey's path. That's a promise. I will make sure that the next 3 years are hell for you. Got that?"

What? But I wasn't even…my mouth drops open and at first I can't speak. I glance at Simone who just rolls her eyes to the back of her head as Demitry and Mya stalk away.

"I wasn't even talking about Gage," I yell after. "I said Gabe, emphasis on *abe*! Nobody wants your stupid, lame boyfriend anyway!"

"Oh, Ali."

"What?" I yell, turning toward Simone but stopping when I come face to face with [oh dear God] Gage Campbell. Stupid Phy Ed. Why are they all in *my* gym class?! I swallow the lump in my throat but I can't blink. Goodness, why can't I blink? Gage looks me up and down like I'm the cretin that his so-called girlfriend accused me of being. I try to say sorry but suddenly my throat is dry. Gage gives me a look of disappointment, the same one he gave Demitry the day of the kickback, before walking away and catching up to her. Simone steps closer to me and suddenly I'm able to blink again. "Do you think he heard me?" My voice is a total whisper.

She nods slowly. "Yeah, he totally did."

Darn it, Ali and your big, stupid mouth. This type of stuff is only supposed to happen in those goofy "tween" books and movies. Y'know, where everything that can go wrong, does go wrong. This is the real world, so why does it continue to happen to me? The bell rings and I reluctantly head to class. The last thing I need is detention.

Ready. Set. Serve! ●

"Why do you want to do this?" Erika doesn't even look up at me when she speaks. She pushes her glasses higher onto her nose with her index finger and flips a page in her English book.

"I like sports." I'm super nervous and keep rubbing my hands together over and over. I think I might start a little campfire.

"You like soccer."

"I like sports."

She closes the book and exhales heavily and looks at me over the top of her frames. "Let me rephrase. You hate volleyball."

"I don't hate any sport."

"You know what I – Simone. Simone."

Simone answers but doesn't look our way. For the first time I notice she's staring at the other end of the bench. Staring and smiling.

Me and Erika lean forward, then look at each other then look ahead again. Simone wiggles her finger at the boy at the other end. I don't know him but I've seen him around. He's cute I guess. Wild brown hair. Brown eyes. Cream colored skin. I think he's from Sweden or something. When I look over again, he's smiling at her and blushing. Why don't they just say hi and get it over with?

"All the popular girls around here do one of three things. Cheer. Track. Volleyball," Erika continues. "And suddenly you're less interested in joining the Panthers and more interested in becoming a Volley Girl."

"So what are you trying to say?"

"I already said what I have to say." She cracks her book open again and pretends to read.

Okay, so I know what she's getting at. But she's wrong, I don't hate volleyball. I hate the girls that play it. They wear shorts that look like underwear – really tight underwear. And all the guys think they are so hot. I like, totally cannot stand them. And well, that's why I need this. It's the only way to break away from Millie and D'asia. Joining the soccer team will make *me* happy, but if I'm a Volley Girl I'll be popular and no one, not even Demitry Haggardy, can stand in my way.

I so need this.

"Okay, ladies, may I have your attention?" Coach Goode calls out and everyone quickly settles down. She welcomes us and thanks us for coming. Warns us that not every girl will make it but for us to do our best, blah, blah, blah. The usual teacher spiel about how no one's a loser just because they don't get picked. A bunch more stuff is said that I'm so sure no one really pays attention to. Then she takes her seat in the middle of a long table and we're ready to begin.

The sound of the gym door opening and closing jars our already shot nerves, and all heads turn toward the sound. I can hardly believe what I'm seeing. Demitry, Mya, and Kamahla come sauntering in late like they own the place. I just know that Coach is so gonna turn them away. Instead she gives a lame warning, adds Demitry to the list, and says for us to come down when she calls our name.

"Good luck," says Erika.

"Yeah," Simone adds, "break a foot."

"It's a leg, not a foot," Erika says in her usual annoyed tone.

"Well, I don't know, break something."

I'm not sure I'm comforted by any of this. My name is called and I jump up, running down past Demitry and her Goon Squad and I nearly face plant right there in front of everybody. I manage to catch my balance and turn sharply.

"Oops," Mya says. "My bad."

Kamahla and Demitry giggle. I'm really ready to lunge when the Coach gets my attention.

"McKenna, are you here to try out or what? Let's go. Pronto."

I swallow the fight in me and join the team that I'm instructed to. When Demitry's name is called, she's placed with the opposition and I'm so incredibly relieved. I can't wait to destroy her. The way tryouts operate is this: We play several short games. Each time girls from each side will get eliminated until it gets down to the final picks. Then we'll pair up with the actual team and play each other and they'll post who makes it in a few days.

No prob. And I mean that – no prob. I breeze through the first two rounds and nearly take off Kay Dezie's head with my serve in the third. Simone is on her feet cheering. Even Erika gets a little hyped for me. I'm relieved but not surprised when I survive to the final match. I'm kinda surprised though to see Demitry still standing on the other side. At the same time, kinda glad because I can't wait to show off and take something, anything from her. I drop low and lean in, give her my most intimidating look. She does the same. Puh-lease. She doesn't scare me. Not here. Not where sports are concerned. She's not in charge in this place. She can be cut just like anyone else.

"Okay, ladies," yells the team captain. "We're gonna mix things up. Everyone in this row here, I want you to switch with everyone in the row that Jadira is pointing to."

Demitry joins a small group of girls and crosses under the net to my side. This is lame. So lame. I can't destroy her if we're teammates.

Maybe I should protest. But protest what and how? *Excuse me, but she's an evil witch who I don't like and earlier she threatened me and I wanna make her pay, not find a way to work together.*

Demitry takes her position and looks back and rolls her eyes at me. Fine. Whatever. I'll just do my best and make the team. That's what I came here for anyhow, not to do battle with Demitry Haggardy. It's my serve. I set the ball and toss it in the air. Just as I am moving my hand forward to connect the base of my palm with it, in walks Gage and his crew. I'm so caught off guard, I freak and miscalculate, totally missing my serve.

"Wow, Ali. Nervous, are we?" Demitry calls over to me.

"No. I'm fine. I missed. It happens."

"Yeah, it does. Now cut the bickering and just don't let it happen again," says the co-captain, adding to my now frazzled nerves.

I take a deep breath, set and serve as expected. The ball covers the net a couple times. We almost lose it but a sophomore already on the team sacrifices her body to recover it and shoot it over. The ball is returned and is coming right for me. I move in for the save. This is perfect. I get to show them that I'll be an asset. I have good instincts and reflexes. I run forward and brace myself for the return when –

"Point, B Team!" cries some redhead girl who's only job is to keep score.

Jadira, the co-captain looks pretty ticked. "How'd you miss that, freshie. It was delivered right to you."

"Yeah, Ali. How'd you miss that?" Demitry asks, snidely. She's not actually expecting an answer. As a matter of fact, she knows how I missed it.

"You pushed me, that's how!"

"Did not."

"Did too!"

"Prove it."

"Cut it out you two," Jadira scolds, "or you're both getting benched."

My jaw is clenched so tight. If I could, I'd serve that ball right into the back of Demitry's stupid head. We rotate and I'm so glad that we're in different rows because it's becoming harder and harder not to attack her.

"You *do* realize he came to see me. Not pathetic little you."

I won't look back at her. I absolutely refuse to look at her. But she's making me mad. I'm so mad that I feel my shoulders shake and when the ball comes in my direction I fumble and just barely pass it to the girl beside me. Good thing she's able to recover because the last thing I need is another warning from Jadira. The other team probably thought I would miss and didn't recover in time, giving us the point. I'm relieved as they get scolded by Captain April.

Demitry giggles and leans toward An'Drea Carter. "Oh my gosh, Ali McKenna almost ruined it for us. She's such a weez. Midgets shouldn't even be allowed to play sports. Their little arms and legs are too small to ever do anything useful!"

An'Drea looks me over, shakes her head, and laughs along. I turn away and roll my eyes so hard, I actually fear that they'll stick. I have got to ignore her. Being a Volley Girl is so much bigger. Just be cool, Ali. It'll all be over soon. I steady myself and breathe carefully, calming myself. I try to shift my vision so I can see what's coming at me, but keep Gage and the pop kids out of it…but they're right there and I swear they're looking at me. Least it feels like they are. Gage leans into Anthony Patterson and whispers something, casually pointing a finger and they all laugh.

Okay, Ali, don't be paranoid. You're up again. Save the ball and if we can hold out and win this rally, we'll be good until the team votes. I got this one. Perfect. Per –

"Ah!" What the –

"Oh my goodness, Ali, I'm sorry," Molly Morris cries, reaching to help me out.

And then it happens. While I'm crashed onto the floor with Molly rushing in to try and pull me to my feet, Demitry seems to float above us in slow motion. Her golden brown skin is glowing, and her long ponytail carries with the wind. Her form is pure perfection – just like her connection. She spikes the return, winning the rally and the short match for our team.

All the girls cheer and gather around Demitry. Even Molly seems to forget that she nailed me and sent me hard to the floor. Jadira is like a proud mother hen, telling her how great her save was. People are saying crap to her like, how she's a natural and how she'll probably be made varsity. She robbed me, can't they see? I know what she did. She purposely shoved Molly into me so she could sabotage my effort and save the game.

I push through the girls. "You did that on purpose, I know it was you."

"Did what? Win the game that you almost cost us?" She twists her stupid pouty lips to the side. "Yeah. I totally did that on purpose. That was the point of all this – to separate winners...from losers."

"So you admit it. You cheated."

"We're on the same team, silly. How can I possibly cheat?"

"You know what you did, Demitry."

"And what exactly are you accusing me of, Ali?"

"You pushed Molly into me so you could get the save. Molly, tell them!"

"Well...I don't know...maybe the push was a little hard but, I don't think...," Molly stammers uselessly.

And Demitry has the nerve to look shocked. "You are such a schizo. Why would I do that? And if I did something so very risky and courageous, it would have been totally done for the team. I mean, maybe we were all afraid you wouldn't be able to reach a ball coming that high."

I react without thinking. The big moment of regret. I don't actually mean to attack Demitry. Something else takes over and suddenly we're on the floor and she's trying to push me away.

"Get off me, you rodent," she screams.

And I scream back but not actual words. Really nothing coherent at all. Just a series of sounds of different pitches that form together and equal gibberish.

"Someone get her off me!"

A bigger crowd forms. I can't see anything but Demitry Haggardy beneath me, but I can sense the blood lust. Someone grabs me and I feel myself being pulled back but I don't think I'll ever have the courage to do this again and I am so not ready to back down.

"Ms. McKenna, let her go." That's definitely the coach. Oh crud, the coach! Well, all bets are off! I can't back down now.

"Alijah, stop it," I hear Erika yell. "You'll get detention."

"Hit her. Hit her good." That's definitely Simone.

"No, Simone, she can't hit her. Her mom will totally freak out on her if Ali gets sent home for actually hitting someone."

Mom! I let Demitry go and sit upright. I was right, there is a crowd and the first face I see amongst it is Gage's and it looks really, really disappointed. I have to get out of here.

"Look out," a voice cries out.

People depart. I glance around to see what's going on and when I look up –

"Not again," I groan, trying to sit up on the nurse's cot. Nurse Morris hands me a cold compress and I put it in the center of my forehead and collapse again. "What happened?"

"What do you recall?" the nurse asks me.

"Volleyball tryouts. Demitry Haggardy. Someone yelled."

"Your mom is on her way to get you and take you home."

"Did I make the team?"

"I don't know, Sweetheart."

I sigh and look away. I turn back toward her. "Am I suspended?"

She gives me a sympathetic look. "I don't know. Probably."

I groan and start to wonder exactly what's happening to my life. Suddenly I find myself actually missing the days of Arthur Ashe.

Meh-He-Kana
(y'know, people from Mexico)

💋 Robust

"I don't wanna go to school today."

I'm sitting on Mom's new loveseat, the one she bought herself as a gift for not only getting her hours back but getting a promotion. I'm looking out at the mountain of snow that formed overnight. Forlornly, that's how I look at the cold white stuff. It's also today's Word of the Day. Desolate or dreary. Unhappy or miserable as in feeling, condition, or appearance. There, I used it. Mentally but I used it nonetheless so Mom should be happy.

"You're going to school, Alijah. That's the end of that." Mom is busy packing a snack bag for Maddex while Laurence puts the finishing touches on her lunch. It's kinda sweet that he does that for her, I guess.

"But I don't feel good," I whine.

"You feel fine." That's not Mom, that's Millie and my attempt to legitimately be excused from the torment of the day is so absolutely not her business.

"You don't know how I feel," I say, spinning around in the seat so I can eyeball her directly.

"You just want to stay home so you can play in that stupid snow like some stupid little kid. Grow up, Ali."

Okay, so to be clear, I don't really want to stay home as some sort of protest against the snow but rather in honor of it. I love snow. The best part about being a kid growing up in the Midwest *is* snow. And just because Millie thinks fourteen is too old for snowboarding, snow angels, and building forts to throw snowballs from, doesn't make it true.

"*You're* stupid and you need to mind your own stupid business."

"That's enough," says our mother.

"Mom, your daughter just called me stupid."

"You called me stupid first."

"I didn't call *you* stupid, Stupid. I said you're acting stupid."

"Mom!"

Our mother slams her palm hard on the counter and we both jump to attention. "I said it's enough. You *both* sound quite unintelligent right now. Millicent, where is your little sister? The bus will be coming in ten minutes and she hasn't eaten her breakfast."

"She's not feeling good."

"*Well*, Millie. She's not feeling *well*."

"Oh, well," Millie mumbles sarcastically, rolling her eyes as she turns away.

"Mom, Millie rolled her eyes at you." Naturally I'm not an

unprovoked tattle but she started it.

"Did not."

"Did too."

"Girls," Mom yells. "Please. It is much too early for this. Now, Ali, get your things and get ready to head to the bus stop. Millie, I hope you don't think you're driving. You're taking the bus, too."

"What? Why?" Millie squeals like the big baby that she is.

"I also need you to come directly home from school today to take care of D'asia."

Wait, what? D'asia gets to stay home, is that what I'm to understand? I open my mouth to speak but Millie's brattyness cuts me off.

"Not fair. I have to skip practice because D'asia got some stupid illness? And why can't I drive my car? It's mine and I don't wanna sit on some stupid smelly bus with stupid smelly underclassmen."

"Millicent Ezan, I am going to strongly suggest that you find a synonym for the word stupid and quickly. Now, not that I need to explain myself to my child, but it is the first snow and you are an inexperienced driver - "

"Whose fault is that?"

"Excuse me."

Uh oh. So, it was my intention to dispute the fairness in D'asia being allowed to stay home just cause she claims she doesn't feel good when I'm expected to go to school sick [so what, I'm not really sick but still]. But now, I'm just going to grab my bag and get ready to go. Mom didn't say excuse me in a way that says *I didn't hear what you said. Please repeat that.* No. She said it in a way that says, *I hope I didn't hear you correctly and I dare you to repeat that if you value your life.*

"I'm just saying - " Millie opens in defense. Wonder where she's going with this. " – if you would have let me get my car last year like you promised – " Aha! So that's where!

"That's it! A week. Hand over the keys."

"What? No."

PAUSE. Did Millie just tell my mom, no?

"No?"

"I mean –"

"Did you just tell me no?"

"Yes. I mean, no! I mean…"

"Two weeks. Keys. Right now!"

I almost feel sorry for Millie. Tears are starting to fill up the corner of her eyes and I almost feel sorry for her. But then I remember how she sold me out with Mom only minutes ago, totally not backing my play to stay home and enjoy the one little pleasure in my dreadful teenage life. Who cares if D'asia is staying home? Millie has to take the school bus for 2 whole weeks. Sometimes life is fair!

I pat the snow in my hand as tenderly as possible, trying my best to make the most perfectly round snowball that I can. But my efforts are futile. It's just too fluffy to be effective. I pat and mold one too many times and the white stuff crumbles in my mittened hand.

"I hate the winter. Did I mention how much I hate winter?" Erika frowns and dusts away the cold flakes that have floated from my hand to her new blue pea coat. "The cold. The dreariness. The barren trees?"

"You mentioned it," Simone says in a totally-over-it tone.

"Well if I failed to make mention of how much winter sucks before now, just know that I hate how bad winter sucks."

I bend down and pick up a fresh batch of snow and make another awkward attempt at forming a weapon. "You mentioned that too. Now please stop mentioning it before I put this snow down the back of your coat and give you another reason to hate winter."

"You wouldn't dare."

"Or would I?"

She squints her eyes and steadies herself before me. I squint back and steady myself as well. This thing between me and Erika, it's nothing new. Happens every winter for as long as I can remember. She's always talking about how when she grows up she's moving to a tropical island. I'm never leaving the Midwest. I love it here. Sure, I'll travel but this will forever be my home.

"You're both idiots," says Simone, knocking the snow from my hand.

"Hey!"

"Well, cut it out. You know how much she hates winter," Simone says, finishing her statement in total sarcasm. She steps away and stares in the distance. I look to Erika who stares back at me before we both look in the direction Simone's gazing in. "What are they doing to that girl?"

"Who is she?" Erika questions and Simone and me just shrug.

I feel for the girl walking toward us. She's a big girl – a very big girl, and Mya and two others that I recognize as being friends with Demitry Haggardy, are following close behind and tossing snow in her hair.

"That's it. That's it," Erika cries.

"Are you gonna say something to them?" I ask in a sorta panic, though I can't figure out just why I feel so panicked. What they are doing is wrong and someone should stand up to them. It just... well, it shouldn't be us.

"*We're* going to say something to them, Ali."

"*We* don't even know her," Simone says.

Aah, the voice of reason. I have enough high school woes without making even more A-Group enemies.

"We don't have to know her. We know what those stupid girls are doing is wrong."

Erika starts to walk in the direction of the bigger girl and the spawns of the Devil that are trailing her but I catch her wrist before she can make it too far. I didn't mean to but...well, maybe I did. I mean, on that whole subconscious level, y'know. We're already practically social outcasts. Do we really want to dig the hole deeper? And so I present this to her as if I think she'll really care.

"Ali, I don't care. That's you and Simone's thing. All I care about, where this high school experience is concerned, is creating and maintaining an academic record strong enough to get me into Dillard University."

"Dillard University?" Me and Simone mouth to each other in total confusion, completely spacing on the poor bullied girl Erika sought to rescue mere moments ago.

"Dillard...in New Orleans?" She waits and watches us but we

have no clue what she's talking about. "HBCU? Founded during the Civil War...to prepare the newly-freed slaves for going into American society? Oh my goodness, you two are the...the...grrrr!"

I shrug. I've never heard of Dillard but I have heard of social cliques and their importance during high school. And she is so about to destroy us.

"The bus," Simone calls after Erika who is already charging in the girl's direction and starting the process of jumping to her defense.

I groan and shake my head, looking to Simone for moral support. We can't do this, we just can't. We don't even know this girl and furthermore, we have no clue if she needs or even wants our help! Sadly, Simone jerks her head toward Erika, signaling that we have to follow. We have no choice. We're her best friends and the BFF Code clearly states that so long as laws are not being broken, whatever the situation, we're all in it together.

"...guys are so pathetic and you really need to grow up. How would you like it if someone treated you this way? Do unto others, ladies. Do unto others. You know the rest." This is the statement Simone and I walk in on. I could just die.

"Oh my god. Hilarious. Guys, check it out. We're getting scolded by an AP geek and her friends Tiny Tammy and the Pillsbury Dough Girl," says the one I recognize as Amanda Curry. She's as mean as Demitry, if not worse. All she needs is a boyfriend with enough rank and a parent with connections and she certainly could be a contender for taking Demitry's spot as Wilma Rudolph High's Queen Bee in Training.

I glance sympathetically at my friend. She's so obviously hurt but she tries to suck it up. She's sensitive about her size. Simone's not fat by any means, but she's definitely big for her age.

"Look at her," chimes in the other girl whose name I don't know. "No wonder she's running to this blimps aid, she's like, three rolls away from being the Michelin Man herself."

My cheeks are so hot that if anyone touched them, they would so get burned. I don't think. Just react, flinging the snow I've been holding in my mittened hands but I'm too late. Instead of hitting one of the mean girls, the white stuff spreads across Mrs. Dutchwood's fake fur coat. The snickers heighten my embarrassment.

Mrs. Dutchwood dusts her coat off, eyeing me with aggravation. "Break it up, ladies, and get to your buses now before I have all of your parents up here pleading their case about why their kid shouldn't get a weeks suspension. Am I clear?"

She scolds all of us, victims alike but mostly focuses on me. I back down…unwillingly but the last thing I need is for Mom to get yet another phone call from school about how I assaulted a teacher with snow. This isn't about the unknown girl. I can't believe Erika even put us in this mess. But now that we're in it, I'm not going to put a desire for acceptance and popularity above my bestee for life. No way.

"Give *us* suspension?" Erika can't seem to let injustice, any injustice, go. "Do you even care what is going on here on school grounds?"

Mrs. Dutchwood sighs. Her nose is beet red and starting to run. She looks tired, worn down really. "No, I don't care. You'd like to know what I care about? Being home in front of my fireplace with a warm body, dry nose, cocoa in my favorite mug and my favorite pink Snuggie. Now unless you are willing to find out how really little I care right now, I suggest you ladies get to your respective buses and find your way home. You can finish your little feud some other time, and I'm so sure you will, but not on my time."

And with that, she turns away, bent on yelling at some other poor, innocent souls just trying to do the right thing by their fellow students.

"This isn't over, losers," Amanda says as she shoves past the girl who, in my opinion, started all of this.

"I can't stand those girls," I hear Erika say as I, foolishly, gaze into the distance after them. "Are you alright?"

"Yeah…yeah I'm fine," I answer absently before I turn around and realize that she's not talking to me.

"Yes, I'm *great*," the girl answers sarcastically. "I get humiliated on my first day by girls I don't even know and yay me, here comes The Skinny Girl Super Hero Squad to the rescue to make it all better."

"I was only trying to help," says Erika.

"Wait - me too? You think *I'm* a skinny girl," Simone asks, smiling inappropriately.

The girl gives an eyeroll accompanied by the kinda chuckle that means you're disgusted about something. "Thanks but I can take care of myself." She walks away before Erika can utter another word, but after a couple steps she stops and turns back our way. "Thank…thank you…for at least trying. No one ever does that."

We watch as the girl continues to walk past the yellow school buses. Erika, who now isn't so sure she did the right thing [maybe she'll listen to Simone and me in the future] signals for us to follow, and guides the way to the bus that will take the three of us home.

I hate lockers. Just one more thing that I have to share. At Wilma Rudolph, if you're fresh meat, your locker partner is assigned. Why the stupid school assigns your locker partner, Idk. Personally, I think it's stup – oh my gosh, I do use that word lots. Mom was actually right about something. Fine. I think it's dumb. I can pick my own partner. But for freshies, they make us team up with who they choose for us. Something about getting to know someone outside your inner circle. I don't need to get to know anyone outside my circle, I know enough. It's small, simple, and sweet and I prefer it that way – okay, so I don't but for now anyway, it's easier. I'm not having much luck with outsiders these days.

Tyson Finch is my partner and he's such a lame and even worse, a slob. He thinks he's so handsome 'cause he's got those green eyes and curly hair and he lifts weights like, all the time. He's an annoying meathead and not very bright. I knew this at Arthur Ashe. I didn't need to be reminded of how much he sucks at Wilma Rudolph and especially not by sharing my locker with him.

Now, here he is, leaning against Megan Bradley's locker and staring at me while open-mouth munching on a thirty-five cent bag of Flaming Hots. I wish he would just go away.

"Do you eat?"

I pause from looking for a space to put my Algebra book and glare at him. "What kinda stup – dumb, what kinda dumb question is that? Of course I eat."

"Then why you so little?"

"I don't know. I just am. A little thing called genetics. You probably wouldn't know what that is since you slept through

Biology."

"I know what genetics is. What about Millie's genetics? She ain't little like you. She tall and she fine. She model, right?"

"She has a different – you know what? Why am I talking to you? You don't matter."

"You know you like me. You wanna be my girl?"

"What?" *What?!*

Tyson crumples the now empty bag and rudely tosses it to the floor. I open my mouth to complain [I loathe litterbugs] but before I can blink, he's in my face sucking the red hot off his fingertips. I cringe.

"Look, you cute. You too small for my taste but you still cute."

"And your point?"

"My point is, I know you like my boy Gage."

PAUSE. How does *he* know? Okay, so now my spine stiffens. I don't mean for it to. Am I obvious? Because I'm so about to lie and say I don't like Gage at all so I hope my body language doesn't betray me.

"What are you talking about? I don't like Gage." There, I said it. Said it like a bad actress in a low budget film. Was I convincing?

Tyson laughs and shakes his head before taking a step closer. I step back but bump into the person behind me. I turn to offer an apology but the guy just scowls and mumbles something inaudible preceding the word freshman. I don't know why upperclassmen are like that. It's like we're diseased or something. They were freshmen once too, though they choose to forget. I mumble my sorry anyway and turn back to face Tyson who is now so close I can almost taste the Cheetos he just ate.

"Here's the deal. We're locker partners so I care about you. Sweetest Day is coming up and we both know half the female freshman class is gone be all over ya boy leaving notes and flowers and cards and stuff at this locker. It's only gonna make you feel jealous and even more lonely than you obviously are."

What in the world? Is that the vibe I've been sending out? Maybe Tyson isn't the lame, maybe I am.

"So, what are you proposing?" I ask while trying my best not to inhale. There's something more on his tongue than Flaming Hot Cheetos and the combo is bordering on vomitrocious. What do girls see in him?

"I make you my girl. We play the role, hold hands and kiss in the hallways. Y'know, show everybody that you can pull a fly dude like myself. That way your stock goes up."

"My stock?"

He sighs and I nearly faint. Is my face green? Must be. Fortunately his frustration leads him to take two steps away. "Your stock, girl. You know, that thing that makes you interesting to the opposite sex. Now, I'm not saying you'll be Gage Campbell status so soon but, y'know, you'll be closer than you are right now."

I nod slowly. I can't believe I have to spend another six months with this guy. And suddenly, to my great relief, an arm loops through mine and I see Simone's hand come across and slam the locker closed.

"She'll keep your generous offer in mind. Right now, we're late for study. See ya, Tyson."

"Oh, okay. See ya. Hey, if she don't want to do it, I can pass the offer on to you, Simone," he calls out after us as we rush down the hall. "I love me some thick girls!"

Simone and I shudder at the same time.

"What do these silly girls see in that fool?"

I shake my head slowly. "Pretty green eyes."

"He's such a goober, oh my gosh. Anyway, I'm totally starving. I hope there's something good on the menu today for a change. I missed breakfast because my mom was being such a spaz and a lame and I just had to get out of the house. Then I found a bag of Doritos in my bag and only ate like one or two before Mr. Pennington totally busted me and made me throw them away or get detention. I almost took detention because I was so hungry. But then my mom would have been even more spaztastic so I – Ali look."

We stop short and see the girl that we further sacrificed our rep to try to protect the other day being teased by the same stupid girls. She ignores them, or pretends to. I mean, how can you really ignore someone when they're embarrassing you in front of everyone?

"Isn't that the same girl from the bus stop?" Simone asks.

I nod. "Yeah, it's her. Should we say something?"

"Yeah, right. Erika's not here. So what's the point of making a fool of ourselves for some girl we don't even know?"

I consider this. If Erika was here the decision would be made for us. But Simone is right, look what happened last time. We brought unnecessary attention to ourselves, almost got into a fight and nearly got our parents called. And the girl didn't even appreciate it. But I can hear what's being said. They're only teasing her because of her size. Something she maybe can't even do anything about. I know how that feels. In Health class we talked about thyroid issues. It means that no matter what you do you can't help but gain weight or, in some cases, lose it. What if this girl has a messed up thyroid?

"I'm going to say something."

Simone grabs my arm and snatches me back before I can get anywhere significant. "Are you out of your mind? Do you not remember the other day? You thought Erika was foolish and now you wanna be an idiot, too? No way. This isn't our business."

"C'mon. Maybe Erika was right. It isn't fair and everyone is just standing by and laughing at her. I know what that's like. We both know what it's like."

Simone tenses and her cheeks blush. I hit a sore spot though I hadn't meant to. Or maybe I had. I needed to appeal to her sympathetic side. She starts to say something to me but instead just looks up at the ceiling. "I have a test later. I'll meet you in study hall."

I call after her but she waves me off and keeps on walking. So I'm on my own, left alone to swoop in like High School Hero and save someone else's day, a move that can destroy mine. What am I thinking? Simone is right. It's not my business and I should leave well enough alone and join her for study.

But, for some reason, I'm walking in the wrong direction and saying words that can't possibly be coming from me. "Hey! Why don't you three pick on someone your own size?" I ask as I stop in front of Mya Foster. Why did I just say that? Oh gosh. That made no sense. It's like, whose side am I on anyway. But that's what the tough guys in the movies *always* say and it sounds good when they say it.

The girls look to one another and then back to me before bursting out in laughter. My cheeks are burning and all I wanna do is run and hide under the table Simone selected for us.

"Aaand, who exactly would that be? You?" says a girl that I don't know, and they all laugh more.

Mya takes a step closer. "You are sooo lame, Ali. Demitry has been right about you all along."

Amanda chuckles and looks me up and down. "Good one, McKenna. Maybe Mya and Demitry are wrong. Maybe you're not so lame after all. Or, maybe you're so lame you don't even know how to defend the charity cases you deem worthy of standing up for. C'mon guys, lets go. Gage is waiting and I heard pizza pockets are on the menu. We might wanna get one before Queen Kong beats us to it."

They laugh hysterically as they walk away. I stand with my back to the mystery girl, mortified and afraid to look at her. Maybe I should walk away, too.

"Thanks a lot," she says.

I exhale and turn to face her, relieved and thrilled that she appreciates my efforts. "You're welcome. It was my pleasure. I can't believe I actually stood up to them. That was so awesome. I just thought what those stupid girls were doing –"

The sound of her locker slamming hard startles me. "I was being facetious you idiot, or do you even know what the word means. You skinny girls are all alike. All size zero jeans and size zero brains to match."

She adjusts her bag on her shoulder and walks away. I stand dumbfounded. Did she just insult me? After I put my neck on the line for her, why would she insult me? Okay, so I inadvertently insulted her but I hadn't meant to. What happened to it being the thought that counts?

"Hey. Hey," I call out after her and jog to catch up. "Now wait, I didn't have to get involved. Those girls are the idiots and I was just trying to –"

"Trying to what? Make a bigger fool of me than they were? You're right, you shouldn't have gotten involved. I don't need your help. I don't even know you."

"I'm sorry…okay. I just…I'm not good at this sort of thing. Y'know, stepping in when I see injustice. That's my friend Erika's deal. But Erika wasn't here and Simone got mad at me and…it's just…well, I know what it's like."

"You know what it's like. Good one."

"If you stop feeling sorry for yourself for one second and peek outside of your own messed up world, you'll see that I'm not exactly their size either. So yes, I know what it's like."

She stops walking but doesn't look at me. I stand behind her. Now this is awkward. I don't know if I should keep standing here or go on to class. I hate this. Bet I won't defend anyone else ever again.

"Fine. Thank you."

I groan and roll my eyes. "Don't worry, it'll never happen again."

She turns to face me just before I walk away. "No…thank you. No sarcasm. That took guts. What you said, that was pretty stupid but…well, I guess I'm glad you said anything at all."

Now this is much better. I look up to her and smile. She's pretty with blushing red cheeks and dark eyes with dark liner that makes them pop.

"I'm Nathalie. Nathalie Flores."

"Ali McKenna. Hey, I'm heading to study but I got lunch after. If you're on lunch at the same time you're welcome to join me."

"Oh, so cause I'm fat you think I'm just looking for the first opportunity to eat."

Omg, I've done it again! "No, no of course not. It's just that you're new and I figure if we have the same lunch hour we could –"

"I'm kidding. I'm kidding," Nathalie says, laughing. I feel like I wanna throw up but I fake like I'm relaxed and smile. "Thanks but I'm pretty behind with starting the school year so late and all. I'm just gonna head to the library during lunch and do some make up work. Maybe next time. Nice meeting you, Ali McKenna."

She turns and walks away before I can say what I'm thinking. Make up work? I didn't know anyone besides Erika and D'asia would actually do that. And she's getting picked on for *weight?* I shrug it off and hurry to join Simone before I find myself locked out.

 Grrrr...age!

Something is different about D'asia, I just know it. I don't care what anyone says, it's true. I can't tell you exactly what it is. Maybe she's even taller. Maybe her breasts have grown more. Is her hair longer or her skin even clearer than ever? I'm not certain but whatever it is, I don't care for it.

I'm the second oldest. Why can't I be taller with bigger boobs? Or maybe those aren't a factor in her change at all. But something sure has her spine straighter, her twins perkier, and her face glowing, and I think I know just what it is. Okay, so I'm not all that perceptive and I really had no idea until Auntie Donna pointed it out. Boys! That's what it is – maybe. Auntie Donna says that boys'll make hair grow in places there was none. I'm not exactly sure what she means by that but I'm pretty certain that I don't wanna know.

Millie says I know but I'm naïve. So be it.

I believe Auntie Donna about the boys theory but as far as I know, D'asia's only been seeing one boy. But Auntie was very specific. She said boys plural. I don't know who the other boys are that make up the oh so important S at the end of their description, but I intend to find out.

"Why are we –"

"Shhh. Keep your voice down," I whisper to Simone.

She sneers at me and I roll my eyes.

"What do you think you're gonna find out?" Erika whispers.

"I don't know."

"Alijah Dominique McKenna. It's freezing out and I let you talk me into missing the school bus for some silly rogue mission? I thought you wanted to tryout for Drama Club."

"Don't be silly. I'm no actress and besides, Drama Club tryouts were last week."

Simone pinches me hard on my side. I want to cry out but instead I bite my lip. I glare at her and she glares in return. We're here, in the auditorium hiding backstage because D'asia told Mom that she would be staying after school today for Drama Club tryouts. Like I told Simone, tryouts were last week. Clearly she's up to something and I wanna know what it is. She doesn't tell me anything. She conspires with Millie and leaves me in the dark. That's going to end today.

"Really, Ali," Erika sighs. "What's going on?"

The sound of D'asia's voice catches my attention. "Shush." I creep forward carefully and ever so gently pull the heavy red curtain aside enough that I can see her. I hear a voice, a male voice, but

I can't tell who it belongs to and I can't see him without risking exposing myself.

"Is that D?" Simone asks me. I wave her off. "Ali, is that D'asia?"

I turn sharply, glaring again. Goodness, doesn't she understand what a good glare means? Obviously not because she keeps speaking.

"Who's she with?"

"I don't know. Can't see him."

"Well let me look."

"I got this."

"Obviously not if you don't know who is out there."

"Hush," I say with finality and turn back toward the curtain.

D'asia giggles and the sound makes my stomach turn. I wish a boy would make me giggle. Maybe I'll call Millie's brother Gabe later and see what he's up to. Ever since he met his new girl friend Callie [as in friend that is a girl], he doesn't talk to me as much. I can hear their footsteps as they get closer to the stage.

"...and you're so pretty," the male voice says.

I stop breathing. Literally stop breathing. My face feels like it should be blue from the lack of oxygen. I now know who my sister is talking to, who she's giggling with. But it can't be. It's not possible. I strain to see without revealing myself. I can hear Erika and Simone whispering questions behind my back but I try my best to tune them out.

"My sister likes you," D'asia says.

Blood and daggers, that's what I see. She's dead meat.

"Millie?"

"No, silly. Ali. Don't you think she's pretty?"

"Yes, she's pretty." He thinks I'm pretty? He thinks I'm pretty! "But, no offense, she's also pretty weird. And sometimes I think she may be stalking me. Our paths cross way too much for it to be purely coincidental. And she doesn't even speak, just stares at me. It's creepy."

My eyes sting and I swallow hard. I feel someone's hand caressing my back.

"Yeah, she is pretty weird sometimes," D'asia agrees. "But it's okay, girls are weird. She's also nice."

"She didn't seem very nice when she attacked Demi at volleyball tryouts. That was so not cool or called for."

D'asia giggles. "I'm sure Demitry deserved it. She's a pretty horrible person and I'm not exactly sure what you see in her. Ali has a bad temper at times. She could use anger management classes actually…totally, but really she isn't a bad person."

My eyes widen. I can't believe this. What is going on? Is my little sister trying to help me out or steal my boyfriend? Okay, so he's not my boyfriend yet but how can he be if she makes me out to be some weirdo, violent psychopath? I think I've heard enough. This was a mistake; I gotta get out of here.

"Like I said," Gage continues, "she's weird."

D'asia chuckles at my expense. "You just have to get to know her better."

"I'd rather get to know you better."

So I was gonna leave but now they have my attention again. What's going on here? I turn back, returning to my peephole. D'asia is standing and smiling stupidly [yes, I said it – stupidly] and then, here he is. Gage steps forward and into plain sight. His hand to my baby sister's cheek and he's going to…he's…going to… KISS HER!

I don't want to see this, I can't bear it. I turn to run away but my foot gets caught in a cable. I twist about and turn and kick as gently as possible trying to break free but I just make it worse. Simone and Erika try to steady me so they can help but I'm not being very cooperative, I know.

"Gage? Little McKenna?" I pause at the sound of the new voice in the space. Is that Demitry Haggardy? Oh crap. If it isn't one thing, it's something worse. I gotta get out of here. I try to pull free but before I can stop myself, I am being pull down, right through the curtain and out onto the open stage for Gage Campbell, Demitry, D'asia, and all the present world to see.

I'm horrified. Worse, mortified. All eyes are on me and all I can think about is how even more weird Gage must think that I am. His eyes come to mine before turning to D'asia and shaking his head as if to say *I told you so* and I only want to cry. The hurried sound of footsteps travel from behind the dumb red curtain that I'm trapped between and come to me but I can't seem to look away.

Simone takes my hands and helps me to my feet while Erika quickly untangles me. D'asia whispers my name softly and my eyes move to hers. I could kill her, I could just kill her for betraying me like this. But I can't speak. It's too much. All eyes are on me, I'm beyond humiliated and it's all too much. Without thinking, I run across the stage and down the steps. I just gotta get out of here. The sound of Mya and Kamahla's laughter cuts through me. Demitry barely looks my way. I think she's just as embarrassed as I am after catching Gage and D'asia nearly liplocked.

I run as fast and hard as I can until my legs can't take it anymore.

The Pact

A li, your sister is speaking to you," Mom says. I close my eyes tightly and count backwards from fifty. I hear the not-so-little traitor but I would much rather not. With any luck she'll give up and leave me be. "Alijah, answer her. Really, this silent treatment has gotten pretty old and pathetic."

D'asia is doing this on purpose. I know her. Well, I know her as well as can be expected since anything remotely relevant about her personality she shares with everyone except me. Oh no, not with Alijah "Ali/AJ" Dominique McKenna. Millie knows her and Erika knows her and even Simone can say she knows my sister better than I do. Because a month ago I would have never in a million years thought that she would have betrayed me the way she did by nearly kissing Gage Campbell. MY GAGE CAMPBELL!

I glance up from the bowl of Honey Nut Cheerios that I've been hovering so closely to that I'm surprised there isn't milk on my face. My eyes meet the sternness in my mothers and it takes all the discipline that I can muster not to roll them. Not at her directly but that's likely how she will take it. I plaster on a fake smile and turn to face my younger sister.

"Yes, D?" I put like, total emphasis on D and I can tell this agitates her just a bit. "How can I help you this morning?"

"Forget it," she mumbles and slides off her stool, carrying her half empty bowl to the sink.

I shrug my shoulders and take another scoop of cereal, so completely satisfied with myself. I haven't shared a decent sentence with my sister since the auditorium fiasco and I've preferred it that way. I mean, yeah, so she claims that the reason she was even there with Gage was to try to talk me up but that's not what it looked like to me. Gage was going to kiss her and I saw everything! She insists that she wasn't going to let him kiss her but I mean, c'mon, this is Gage friggin' Campbell. What girl in her right mind wouldn't? Erika says she wouldn't but we all know she's hardly ever in her right mind. And besides, I don't believe her anyhow.

"That's enough," Mom belts out, slamming her palm hard against the island. Maddie, who is sitting beside her in his toddler chair picking Cheerios from milk by hand, jumps and tears stream from his eyes instantly. Mom, hardly noticing, grabs him thoughtlessly but continues without taking her eyes from me. "Now Ali, that is your sister. Your baby sister."

"She's no baby. She's an evil Millie-clone."

"I told you that it isn't what you thought it was. I don't like Gage Campbell!"

"What a croc!"

"Why do I even bother?" she says, throwing her hands in the air and stalking toward the stairwell.

"Stop it right there, young lady," Mom orders, patting Maddie's back in a manner I assume she believes to be comforting but it just looks like she's burping him. "Sit. Now. Beside your sister. Ali, don't you dare get up."

"Mom, you don't understand," I plead.

"Oh, I understand. Or did you conveniently forget that I have six sisters? Count 'em, six so I understand. And when I was 16 years old Nay stole *my* boyfriend."

"Whaaaat?" Okay, maybe this could prove to be a little more interesting than my battle with the mini-beast – at least for now.

"Yes, she did. We'd been dating for just shy of two weeks and here comes Nay Nay, strutting around with her boobies all picked up and poked out and her tight jeans and negative waistline. She's only a year older but she was light years ahead of me when it came to boys."

"Auntie Nay was a skank?" D'asia asks in awe and I laugh before I realize what I'm doing. I immediately clear my throat and refocus. Would hate to show a united front.

Mom gives us a disapproving look but softens it. "She was a little skankish but don't tell her I told you though. I was so ticked at her. I'd been in love with Bookie what felt like forever." *Bookie??* "He was so fine. A Senior and co-captain of varsity basketball. He had some pretty brown eyes and he had a Leisure Curl not an S-Curl like the other boys. So his looked like he had what we considered good hair."

"What did you do?" I asked. "Did you wanna fight her?" I glance at D'asia and she sneers at me.

Mom sighs. "Wasn't much I could do. I did my best to make her life difficult. I tried not speaking to her but she didn't care. So I did mean things like break off the sticks on her favorite bamboo earrings and put Elmers inside her Jordan's."

"Ruthless, Mom," D'asia says and I glance her way curiously.

"Now don't you two go getting any ideas on getting even with each other. There are two of you; there were eight of us. I can handle you two. Remember, I am the queen of ruthlessness."

I ask, "So how did you deal with it? Did you ever forgive her?"

"Of course she forgave her, you bed mite." Millie shuffles across the kitchen floor, jumping in our conversation as if she were a welcome part of it. Typical.

"Millicent, hush." Mom sits Maddie back in his seat and he goes back to picking soggy Cheerios like nothing ever distracted him in the first place. "I forgave her, Ali. It took a little time but at the end of the day I realized that she was my sister and would always be my sister. He was just a silly boy and would probably break my heart anyway, with or without her help. She'd be there for the rest of my life and she'd had my back in the past and even though what she did was hurtful at the time, she'd have my back again."

We sit silently. I don't know what to say or if I should say anything. I know that my mother is right but that doesn't immediately eliminate the hurt caused by what my sister did and it sure doesn't just wipe the slate clean. So the moral of the story is that your sisters can step on you and you have to accept it because they'll always be your sister? I'm not so sure how I feel about that philosophy.

"Mom?" D'asia asks.

"Yes, dear?"

"What happened to the guy?"

Mom smiles broadly and stares up at nothing. I swear her eyes start to water up. "I stole him back, dumped him, made him work for me. Then, eventually, I married him."

"Bookie – " I open.

" – is Dad?" D'asia finishes.

Mom nods and lifts Maddie from his seat again. She instructs Millie to clean up his mess before departing up the stairs. I glance at my sister who glances at me. I don't know if I should really believe her version of what happened but according to Mom's tale, I can end up being Mrs. Gage Christian Campbell at some undesignated point in the future. With that prospect to look forward to, I guess forgiveness isn't so bad.

Hater-Nation

Like I said before, something more is different about D'asia, I just know it. I wish I could put my finger on it. I stand with my back to the lockers staring across the aisle at my sister giggling and flirting shamelessly with Jordan. Supposedly the two are an official item but she hasn't told Mom this yet. She may attend school with Millie and me but officially [in Moms eyes at least...okay, and mine too] she is still an 8th grader and therefore not allowed to date yet. Believe me, I have so considered tattling in return for what she almost did to me. But...*sigh*...I guess if you forgive someone you have to truly forgive or else it doesn't count.

Loud laughter captures my attention and my eyes dart in the direction of the group of girls walking our way. They're all dressed in short shorts and tees with long socks. Blue and gold. Two sets of eyes attach themselves to mine and I swallow hard as the girls frosh/soph volleyball team passes me by. I can't believe they let Demitry on the team and not me. Just because of a little physical altercation that she totally started. It's so unfair!

The slamming locker door jostles me back to attention. Nathalie, or Nattie as we call her, notices my expression and looks in the direction of the chatty chics. She rolls her eyes and walks away with me behind.

"Don't worry about those stupid girls, AJ," *I totally got her to call me by an appropriate nickname!* "Every time you see them you turn completely jeal."

"What? No way. I'm not jealous of those stupid girls." So what, maybe just a little.

Nattie stops and turns to face me. "Yeah, ya kinda are."

"Oh my gosh. They're only frosh/soph anyhow. Had I not attacked Demitry Haggardy and made the team, I am so sure I woulda been made varsity. And had that stupid fight not got me banned from team sports for the school year, I'd totes be playing soccer for the Panthers anyhow."

Nat raises her eyebrow and stares at me before shaking her head and turning away. "You give people too much power over you, AJ."

"Easy for you to say. Everyone is afraid of you ever since you spread that rumor about getting out of jail and being kicked out of every school you've ever been to for incidents of aggravated assault."

"Yeah, that was genius wasn't it?" Her brown eyes twinkle when she says that.

"I guess," I mumble. I try to be careful not to offend her. I mean, she says all that stuff about her is a croc but I haven't known her very long and who knows if any of it is just a little true.

"No one bothers me anymore and Demitry doesn't hassle you as much, does she?"

"No, at least not when you're around."

"Then it's working."

"Except now people think I'm weirder than ever for hanging with you. Well everyone besides the Grubber Crowd, they think I'm cool but I could care less about them."

"Dios, AJ! Por favor, stop worrying about what other people think. Who are you?"

"Excuse me?"

"You heard me. Who are you? Without a popular big sister and an increasingly popular little sister. Without sports. Without Simone and Erika, who are *you*?"

I roll my eyes at this foolishness. But when I open my mouth to speak, no words form. Nattie is waiting. I can answer this. I know who I am.

"Ali," Simone calls as she runs in my direction, waving and totally saving me from myself. "Um, hey, Nathalie."

Nathalie gives a tight smile and nods at my friend. "Hey, AJ, I'm gonna head to the auditorium. We'll finish this conversation later."

"Why don't you just sit with us? Simone doesn't mind."

Simone shrugs. "I don't mind."

"No, but I'm sure *she* does."

Simone's and my eyes follow the direction Nattie's go in. They lead to Erika who approaches us with a scowl on her face. I roll my eyes and shake my head. It's like, every time I get a friend outside of our clique, Erika has an issue with them.

"Hello, Nathalie," Erika says all formal-like.

"Wassup, ese?" Nathalie responds sarcastically.

"Idk what that even means."

"Well then maybe you should stop speaking in acronyms and like, watch more Mexican gangsta films, homes." Nathalie chuckles, rolling her eyes, and turns to walk away. "Catch you later, AJ."

"I don't get you, Erika," I say once Nattie is out of earshot.

"I don't get you. Why are you hanging around someone with a reputation like that? How do you think it makes you look?"

"I can't look any worse than I already do. Besides, since when do you care about appearances? I recall a totes self-righteous Erika Bellflower insisting that it doesn't matter what people think of us."

"I hate to say this but Erika's right for a change," Simone adds and I am oh so flabbergasted. "How can we ever expect to change our image if you're hanging out with a…a…thugette?"

"Oh my god, are you two serious? Nat is not a thug. She just spread those rumors so people wouldn't pick on her about her size. You, Erika, should appreciate that Ms. Let-Me-Run-To-Everyones-Rescue. And since people pick on me all the time about *my* size, I know what that's like."

Erika shrugs my words off while leading the way to the auditorium for the school wide enrichment seminar. "And yet, somehow, you've never resorted to spreading horrible rumors about yourself."

I open my mouth to explain how Nattie's approach wouldn't really work for me being 1/3 her size and Eden Grove native and all, but all that comes out is a shriek from the pain caused by someone stepping on my toes. I jump back and lose my balance. I reach out to try and catch myself on a locker but my arm is too short and I land hard on the floor. Woe is me!

Simone and Erika rush to my side but it's a dark, masculine hand that connects to my own. Okay, I'm dreaming. I must be dreaming. No, this can't be a dream because dreams are pleasant and people look forward to them. No, no, this is a nightmare. This is a total nightmare.

"You okay, Ali?"

I swallow hard as I look into Gage's eyes. I am not going to blow it this time. I open my mouth to respond appropriately –

"Dang, Ali. Why're you always on the floor? Dude, you're too clumsy. You need to work on that," says my s'posed best guy friend, and in front of everybody!

I feel heat flooding my face and look away. "I'm okay," I mumble, easing my hand from Gage's grasp and pushing myself up.

"You sure?"

"I'm fine," I say with finality. I don't look at him. I want to but what's the use? I'm a joke. Everyone knows it. Gage, Demitry, Millie…even my best friends. So what's the point? I'll never get a guy like Gage Campbell to take an interest in me. So really, what is the point?

"Gagey, honey, you should leave the trash on the floor where it belongs," says Demitry as she saunters past, looping her arm through his and pulling him away.

I push myself to my feet, reluctantly making eye contact with Gage when he glances back. I walk away as quickly as possible in the opposite direction of the auditorium ignoring anyone that tries to stop me.

Light Bulbs 😃

I think I hate high school. Really. I mean, it sucks pretty ridiculously so. I once thought that when the 8th grade ended, I would get this fresh start and I'd be a Panther and Gage Campbell would finally notice me – I mean, really notice me. Things would look up. By sophomore year all would be well. Millie would be gone to college or New York or London or someplace far away trying to be the next Tyra Banks, and D'asia…well, she wasn't much of a threat being an AP geek and all.

But as I look around the cafeteria and see everyone laughing and getting the best out of their teen years, I realize just how wrong I was. I see clearly what the next three years hold for me. Stress, humiliation, and a never ending supply of short jokes. I gaze ahead and imagine that Amanda Curry is pointing and laughing. Wait. Am I imagining?

"You got some ketchup on your nose," Nattie says. We've been eating lunch together more often since Erika decided to spend more time in the library in a desperate move to get her GPA up.

"What?" I swipe at my nose and look in horror at the thick red stuff on my fingertips. "Great. Just great."

"Dios, AJ. How many times do I gotta tell you – "

"Yeah, yeah, I know. Forget about 'em. Who cares? I care, Nat. I don't know why but I care. My sister is the top dawg everywhere she goes and now look at my little sister. How can I be the only lame McKenna sister?"

Nattie rolls her eyes and reaches for her backpack and starts digging through. "What you need to learn, AJ, is that people either are or they are not. You can't force something to be if it isn't meant to be."

My eyes focus unconsciously on the book on the table as I try hard to really take in what she's saying. It makes sense…maybe, I dunno. Nat is wise but she just doesn't get it. Or maybe I just don't get it. I tilt my head and look closer at the notebook on the table before her. I reach for it but Nat snatches it away before I can get my hands on it.

"What's that?"

For the first time, I see her blush. Oh my gosh, she's embarrassed! "It's nothing."

"*Big Girls Guide to Being Phat*?"

"Why are you so nosey?"

"It was on the table, I didn't go looking for it. What's it for?"

"Dios, AJ! None of your business!"

I swallow hard and sink further into my seat. I glance around cautiously and see curious, judgmental eyes on me. The heavy sound of Nattie sighing catches my attention.

"A weightloss journal," she says through gritted teeth. Her words are so muffled I don't think I heard her right.

"A weightloss journal?"

"Yes, si! Querido Dios, ¿qué está mal satisfechas con esta chica loca y por que salgo con ella? Geez. Make your jokes, whatev. I've heard it all before."

"First of all, not fair, I have no idea what you just said and I've asked you like, a mil times not to do that to me. Second, is it one of those books where you like, right down your food and exercise and stuff?"

"Yes, McKenna, yes. It's one of those. I'm trying to lose weight, okay. It ain't a big deal. Everyone can't be tiny like you."

"Tiny like me? But I don't wanna be –" I shoot upright in my seat. I have an idea and I think it's a good one. "Wait, does it work?"

"What?"

"Your journal thingy. Doing all that stuff, does it work?"

Nat shrugs. "I guess, sorta. I mean, sometimes I lose some when I'm really keeping track of everything. But it's tough and I forget or I stop caring at times. It all depends."

"You think it can work for me?"

The bell sounds and Nattie stands, tossing her bag over her shoulder while looking at me like I've surely lost my mind as I'm sure I surely sound like I have.

"What are you talking about, McKenna. Why would you need to lose weight?"

I shake my head vigorously and stand. "Gain. You want to lose. I need to gain. You think if I keep a journal and track everything I can gain?"

Several facial expressions pass over her face but no sound actually comes out. She walks and I follow. "That's the dumbest...I mean, AJ no one does...maybe...heck, I don't know. As you can see I never had a problem gaining weight. I mean, I can do that with my eyes closed and my brain shut down."

"You're right," I say enthusiastically.

"Watch it, shorty."

"No, what I'm saying is…well, you know how to gain weight and I apparently know how to lose it."

"Your point?"

"We team up. I help you meet your goal, show you what I do that keeps the weight off and you teach me how to put weight on." Nattie stops abruptly and turns to face me. "Come on, admit it. It's brilliant. You know what habits cause you to gain and I know all about being skinny. So, let's work together. I'll start a weight-gain journal."

"There's no such thing!"

"Of course there is. The concept is the same. The goal is only different. Come on, Nattie, I need this. Please. I'm totes out of options."

"This is ridiculous, you know that right?"

"So ridiculous that is has to work. Please…por favor."

Nat turns away but before she heads to class she says, "Yeah, whatever. Get your journal. We'll start tomorrow."

I haven't smiled this hard since Millie was grounded from her car. Maybe things are gonna start looking up for real this time!

Journalism
(aka the Skinny Girls Guide)

✎ Weight Swap

Nat is sitting across from me on my bed, looking at me looking at her. We've decided that our goals should be similar. Somehow we think that would make things much easier. Fifteen pounds is the amount we've settled on [though I know that secretly Nat's goal is much higher than that].

This is as far as we've gotten. Now what? I mean, I've always been small and according to her the last time she was small was never. I've never thought about what I do to be skinny, I just am. I don't pay attention to what I eat, I don't count calories, and I'm not on any specific fitness routine. Oh my goodness, how will this work?! If I can't help her, why would she help me? Omg, *can* she help me?? I mean, seriously. If I have always been this way and she has always been that way, does she even know what advice to give me on gaining weight? I'm panicking like crazy on the inside. I hope she doesn't notice.

"What is it, AJ? Why do you look like you just swallowed a sour ball whole?"

I exhale heavily. "This was a bad idea, wasn't it?"

"Why do say that? I'm actually kinda psyched about it. It's something I haven't tried. And I have tried everything."

I look down at Nat's weight-loss journal and flip through a few pages. She has everything in here. I land on October 6th and run my finger down the page. On this day she got up early, like two hours before she needed to be at school. She did 10 jumping jacks, 7 sit-ups, ran in place for 3 minutes, and did a squat.

That morning for breakfast she had a meal replacement shake and black coffee. In parenthesis she penciled in a bag of Flaming Hots and two swallows of Marisol's Pepsi. Guess that was some delayed honesty. For lunch she had a small salad, a bowl of grapes and a Diet Pepsi. Dinner was just as boring with a small piece of chicken breast and broccoli. Before bed she did 5 more sit-ups, 4 squats, and more jumping jacks.

My eyes return to hers. "I had pizza for dinner last night."

"So."

"And breadsticks. I had six slices of pizza, more than anyone else and then breadsticks. Laurence likes buffalo wings so we split a 12-piece order. I ate seven of those. Mom hates soda and won't allow it in the house but Laurence enjoys Mountain Dew and whenever we order pizza, she lets him get his 2-liter."

"You had some of that too," she states to which I nod in response. "Oh."

"But you don't eat that way all the time...right?"

I twist my lips and look away thoughtfully. "Well, no, I suppose not. Mom and Laurence cook us healthy dinners most of the week. So…yeah. But I eat lots of crap during the day that she doesn't know about."

"Oh."

"And I don't really workout. I mean, I like sports but I didn't make the team so… I used to play soccer all the time with Justin but now that we're in high school and he has all these new, much cooler friends…well, I don't play much anymore which means I don't really do much anymore."

Nathalie sighs and falls backward onto my pillow. "Did I tell you I was a 10-pound baby?"

"Wow. I mean, no." I was nearly half that according to my mom. I have a visual of Nathalie as a baby next to me as one. Interesting. Kinda looks like Nathalie next to me as a teen.

"My mami cooks really big meals all the time. Breakfast, lunch, dinner. No matter what time of day, it's an event. Food is a big part of my family and my culture for that matter. Everyone is always trying to feed you. Eggs and chorizos, burritos, enchiladas. Abuela is always afraid that I'm going to get skinny and die of starvation so she just keeps feeding me."

"Yeah, I wish my mom was afraid of that. She's always baking skinless chicken. Skinless chicken! Like, that doesn't even make sense. I keep telling her that the fat is like thee best part, where all the flavor is but she just looks all disgusted. Vegetables with every meal, salads and fish, all portioned. I bet if you lived here you'd be super skinny and if I lived in your house I'd be normal." Beans and pork and fat and deep fried tortillas, I'd certainly be normal in no time. "That's it!"

"What's it, AJ? What are we gonna do, swap lives? Like our

families wouldn't notice. We don't exactly look alike."

I jump from the bed in perfect dramatic form. My idea is brilliant. Who needs to be a genius? What good are all those smarts that my sister has if it can't help her practically? I glance toward the door and catch eye contact with Millie who happens by at that moment.

"Weirdo," she offers and continues on her way.

I roll my eyes and return my attention to my guest. "We won't swap homes but we will swap meals."

The room is so quiet for seemingly so long I can hear my heart beating. Nat slowly rises, rolling onto her side and resting the side of her face against her open palm. She brushes away a stray strand of hair and looks at me quizzically.

"So, your bright idea is that, what? We sneak out and take our dinners to each other."

"Well, no, not exactly. It'll be a little tough the first night because we can't eat too much. But we save our dinner and swap at school the next day. That way you'll get healthier food and I'll get –"

"Fattier food. Not bad but that's only one meal a day."

"It's a start."

"True," she answers thoughtfully. "Well, what else?"

"What do you mean?"

"We need more than that. It's a start but what else can we do?"

I open my mouth to let all my brilliance continue to pour out and when none does, I close it and take my place on the bed once again. "The journal," I say.

"What about it?"

"Well, there are some things that are staples in our eating lives, right? You're probably gonna have something fried and fatty tonight and I'm probably gonna have something baked and bland. How about we list the types of stuff we eat regularly and trade lists."

"And then?"

"Then we do what we gotta to follow the list. We write it all in our journals to keep track. Everyday." As an after thought I add, "And weigh ourselves. Then we know if it's working."

"And you think that this'll somehow work?"

"Can't hurt, right?"

Nat shrugs but she's not impressed. "Sure, guess not."

Yeah, why not?

Playing Catch Up

"Is that a pimple?"

"What?" There is no way that I have acne. I never get acne. That's the one thing that my body does right. Maybe my delayed development sucks in the height and curvature department, but it's so totally beneficial where certain puberty issues are concerned – namely blob goblins!

I rush across the locker room, aimed for the nearest mirror. I open my mouth to question where this little oozie is located but close it quickly as it's sooo very obvious. A huge, stretched out piece of flesh sits centered and pus-filled in the space between my eyebrows, ready to explode and drown me in disgust and humiliation at any moment.

"Ewww, McKenna's growing a second head out of her forehead."

Oh great, all I need is for Kamahla and Demitry Haggardy to witness my official initiation into my teenage years. I touch my forehead careful and slowly, like, if I move too fast the thing'll freak out and blow up, killing us all. A sound escapes my insides. It's like a weird squeal or something and I don't know where it came from because I am by nature not a squealer but OMG, there is the potential for volcanic activity on my face!

"Ali, calm down," says Simone, rushing to my aide as the other girls nearby just laugh at my pain.

"Get it off, get it off!"

"I can't. It'll go away on it's own."

"I can't wait for that to happen. How long does that take?"

"Dude, it's a pimple. It isn't the end of the world."

"It's huge."

"Well…y'know, maybe you're making up for lost time."

I scowl. She's making jokes. I'm dying here and she's making jokes. "It's not funny."

"It's kinda funny."

"Simone," I hiss, "you're supposed to be my friend."

"I am your friend but you're being like, so melly these days."

Could this be? The most melodramatic of us all is calling me melodramatic? I turn toward the mirror again to get another look from a different angle. Maybe I am trippin'. Kids get these things all the time, right? Simone has had them and so has Erika, though never this huge and disgusting. Oh crud, I gotta get rid of this thing.

I consider again the prospect of squeezing it between my

thumbs and being done with it all together except I don't know what the repercussions of such an action would be. Instead, I push past Simone and gather my belongs before escaping the torturous sound of pleasure coming from my classmates.

"Where are you going?" Simone calls after me and I swear I hear a chuckle between those words.

"To the nurse, where else?"

"The nurse?" Simone replies. "Don't be silly, Ali. I think I have some concealor in my purse. I'm sure I can cover it up for you."

"Let her go," Demitry chimes in. "It would be so totes terrible if that thing exploded and flooded the school!"

Everyone laughs, even Simone chuckles a little, though she tries to cover it up like she didn't find it funny. But it isn't. I shake my head and leave the locker room and the laughter behind. Life has never been simple for me, what with being the middle child and awkward sibling of a genius and future super model, but somehow this high school experience has trumped it all and I'm really not sure what I ever did to deserve this.

My desires were simple enough, I think – play soccer, grow breasts, get my period, and get Gage to notice me in the process. I mean, maybe if he talked to me longer than 2 seconds while helping me from the floor he'd realize that he actually likes me better than Demitry Haggardy. Instead, I fail at everything I try. Even my weight gain plan is failing me. So far the only place I've gained weight is on my face!

"Ali! Ali, wait up," Simone calls after me.

I turn to face her. It's in this very moment that I realize just how perfect she is. Tall with boobs and hips and great skin. She's likely only my friend because she kinda has to be. I mean, she, me, and Erika have known each other forever, we live on the same block, and our mother's are friends. But if the circumstances of our lives had been different would she even be here right now or would she have stayed behind, laughing at my pain with the rest of 'em?

"What, Simone? Why didn't you stay to crack jokes with your new bestees?"

"My goodness, totes melly and why for? Okay, so I laughed a little, it was funny. I didn't mean anything by it. You're just not making sense being all bent over a stupid pimple. And since when do you let Demitry and her goonettes bully you anyhow?"

"Since uhm, always. Where have *you* been all my life?" How could Simone ask such a question? I mean, seriously. Demitry Haggardy has hated me from since the beginning of time, and I'm not even kidding.

PAUSE and REFLECT. The story of Demitry and Ali goes all the way back to the first grade. My Gran'ma McKenna sent me this gorge dress from Arizona for my 6th birthday. I remember it was all yellow at the bottom, and the top had these real pretty yellow flowers with white flowers around the waist and it tied in the back. It was my fav dress [mostly because it came from out of town]. Well, it was the first day of school and I'm already so nervous right, cause it's like, the first day of regular school ever. And Simone is there and she's already my best friend because of our mom's [Erika didn't move to town until the next year], and that helps kinda but it's still pretty scary.

It was ruled an accident because as we all know everything Demitry does wrong is an accident. The first time that Gage Campbell ever spoke to me was on the playground at recess. He told me that my dress was pretty [as if I didn't already know]. Back then I didn't care. He was a boy and that made him kinda gross. Demitry didn't feel the same, clearly. Nope. Before I knew what was happening I was aiming face first for post rain mud. My hands broke my fall but that obviously wasn't enough to save my dress.

I remember it like it was yesterday. There was this incredible force against my back and I just went flying. And when I turned around, everyone had this look of shock on their face and I could see that they mostly felt bad for me. Everyone except Demitry Haggardy. She was standing right in the middle of it all just staring at me with her cold golden brown eyes.

"Sorry," was her only response. Then she turned and skipped away. Didn't even try to help me up or offer some reasonable explanation and I know why – because there was none. Because she's pure evil, that's why. So Simone's assertion that I was suddenly *letting* her bully me was just a little insane.

"I know all about your sordid history, Al's, but as I recall that wasn't the end of the story. I remember little Alijah McKenna flinging a handful of mud and clocking her in the back of the head instead of taking her crap like you've been doing lately. You never would've let her get away with this back at Arthur Ashe and now you're so desperate to be on her team."

"Yeah, well so were you!"

"True, but not anymore!"

Okay, fine, she's right. I'm just tired of the highlight of my life being the latest battle with the awful girl who has been picking up where Millie leaves off, ruining my life for all of my life. Only I am punished when I fight back. It doesn't change anything. Doesn't improve anything. So what's the point? Life would be better on her team than it's been off of it.

I don't feel like explaining any of this and so I don't. "Please, Simone. Just leave me alone, okay. I'll tell you what, feel free to go back and laugh behind my back with your new friends. You have my blessing."

"You're truly unbelievable. If this is what you've come to be, I hate to see how you'd act if Gage ever did notice you."

I gasp. "You did not just say that."

"Yes I did just say that. And news flash, I meant it!"

"Thanks, *friend*. Thanks for that."

Simone sighs, what I assume to be regretfully, and opens her mouth to respond but I leave and tune out whatever explanation or lame apology she thinks will make it right.

Nattie, Reilly, and me are in my room after school. Nat's doing the last six jumping jacks in a set of fifteen [hey, that's up from a max of ten] while I'm laying across my bed snacking on my second of three churros that she's smuggled into my uber-healthy home. Reilly's on my laptop, bobbing her head wildly to whatever rap song she's playing through Spotify.

I scroll through the numbers in my phone contacts, passing Gabe's name about 16 times, contemplating calling him. We haven't talked in forever. It was like everything was perfect and then he just fell off. Seems things got to be serious with his girl friend who is now his actual girlfriend. Millie just loved offering that tidbit of info to me. No matter. Maybe it *was* creepy to think I could have some sort of future with my older sisters younger brother.

I toss the phone aside and reach beneath the bed as I pop the last bite of the tasty fried dough into my mouth, and pull my school bag from beneath it. I reach in and sift through the books and piles of graded and ungraded papers stuffed inside until I find my designated weight gain journal aka The Skinny Girls Guide. I flip it open to today's date. I need to stay focused on what's most important. If I can alter my body structure, I can change my life for the better and improve my high school experience tremendously.

I reach across to my nighstand for a writing utensil so that I can take note of the pure deliciousness I just ate. The only thing I find is a leadless pencil, no good. I groan. Must everything in my world be a challenge? I fix my mouth to ask Nattie for a pen but she's moved on to sit ups and those are hard enough for her to do without trying to speak at the same time.

I shake my head, grab the last churro, and swing my legs around the bed and jump up. D'asia for sure has something in her room that I can borrow. I tap on her closed door once, then twice. When there is no answer, I decide to walk in and head for her desk. It's perfect [of course] and clear of anything useful.

I find a case of pens in her side drawer but before I take one, a framed photo of my little sister kissing a boy catches my attention. I pick it up and get a closer, wide-eyed look. It's a co-selfie and she's the one holding the phone. How more unfair can life possibly get?

"What are you doing? Why are you in my room?"

I jump, slightly startled, and turn to face D'asia, still holding the photograph in my hand. She charges in my direction and reaches for it but I snatch my arm away.

"Does Mom know what you're out here doing?" I ask sounding quite sisterly if I do say so myself – and I do say so.

"And exactly what is it that I'm doing that's so wrong?"

I give my best authoritative *I'm appalled* look and matching sound effect, though I'm not too sure why. It's not like I didn't know that D'asia was sneaking around with Jordan already, of course they kiss! Still, I'm fuming on the inside. This bothers me more than it should, I know. But lately, it seems that everything bugs me more than it should.

"You're not supposed to be dating and you know it. Just because you're at Wilma Rudolph and you skipped 8th grade doesn't mean you get to skip being an 8th grader. Everything in life can't just be moved up for you just because you have a dumb IQ that's higher than everyone around you."

"What? You're not even making any sense," she says as she gains the upper and snatches the pic from my hand. "Why are you in here snooping through my belongings anyway? Don't you have company to tend to?"

"I wasn't snooping through anything. I needed a pen and where else would I find one in this house but in the room of Geeks-R-Us? Don't change the subject. I think you're getting out of control, D'asia."

"Oh *you* think I'm getting – what in the world is up with you, Sis? You've just been really twisted these past couple weeks."

"You know Mom's rules. Millie had to comply and so do I and just because you got to go to high school earlier than the rest of us doesn't give you a free pass to do whatever it is you want!" My face is warm and probably crimson and I'm breathing a little harder than expected. I inhale deeply and find some composure. I'm actually really confused by my own actions but I've gotta own them now. I exhale sharply and reconnect my eyes to my sister's. "I'm only trying to look out for you."

D'asia pushes past me and returns the photo to the drawer,

none-too-discreetly pushing a pocket folder on top, covering it completely. She turns quickly to face me and before I realize she's even moved, she's hovering above me.

"You're trying to look out for me? You. No. You're just jealous, Ali, that's all. As many rules as you break...have always broken, don't stand here and act all self righteous like you suddenly had an awakening and care about our mother's rules."

"Jealous?" I scoff. "Jealous? Of my *little* sister? You are so full of yourself."

"No, Ali, I think you're the *little* sister now. Jealous. Yes. Because I'm taller, prettier, smarter. Because I have boobs and you don't. Because boys like me, including your precious Gage Campbell. Because I could have him if I wanted him, which I don't because he's actually an idiot jock who isn't into you and only talks to you to make Demitry green, and if you paid a little more attention to studying your books rather than studying what I do, you would realize that. Don't blame *me* for *your* problems. It isn't my fault that you grew up to be lame and I didn't."

I feel like I've been kicked in the stomach with Tammy Palanewski's awful steel toe boots! I try so hard to not show my feelings but all I can come up with to say is, "Whatev." And just in case you think the tortures over, no worries, it's not.

"You're jealous because I'm everything that you wish you could be. Body, beauty, boys. And look at you. Maybe you could get Gage's attention too if you weren't so pathetic these days. Look at you, Ali. Wipe the sugar off your cheek and buy some Clearasil and just maybe you can get a boy to look at you too, then you wouldn't have to be such a hater."

"D'asia!"

I turn to see Millie standing in the doorway. Surprisingly she looks as astonished as I feel. D'asia is supposed to be the good sister, the nice one. I've never heard so much venom come from her. I think I see empathy on Millie's face but then it occurs to me that there is a reason this awfulness feels so familiar.

"You're mistaken, D'asia. You're not *everything* that I wish I was. Millie is the last person that I would ever wish to be."

I turn and push past my older sister without bothering to excuse myself. My older sister who has never been a real sister to me and has now turned my actual sister against me.

"Ali," Millie calls after me. "Look, that was uncalled for. I'll talk to her."

"Don't bother. I think you've done enough already."

"Hold on, are you blaming *me* for this?"

"Of course I blame you, Millie! *You* should blame you. Who else does she sound like?"

Millie shifts uncomfortably and it's almost like she feels bad - almost. "Her going in on you like that was too much, I agree. But it's your fault, Ali, not mine. You're always trying to gain acceptance from other people but *you* don't even accept who you are and now you're jealous of D'asia because of who she's becoming."

"Yeah? And who's that? Millie Junior?"

"No. Secure. You thought because she's younger, somehow she was *supposed* to have tougher breaks. She's supposed to share your insecurities. Well, surprise, she didn't. Wise up, kid sister. How that played out in there was because of tension and animosity that you created, not me."

Millie retreats to her bedroom and slams her door closed before

I can come up with some worthwhile response. I'm not jealous of D'asia and I really wish people would quit accusing me of that. I mean, that's a totally ridic notion, right? What do I look like being jealous of my l'il sister? But Millie embraced her in a way she's never embraced me all because D'asia inherited the Greene genetics and not me. And as the world knows, Millie is shallow and unsympathetic. As a result, D'asia is becoming a royal witch perfectly fit for the Queen of all Witches. That is not jealousy, that is reality.

The sound of the front door opening and Maddie's footsteps running across the floor jar me from my thoughts. I turn to take refuge in my bedroom and remember that Nathalie and Reilly are here when we're suddenly face to face in my doorway.

"Uhmmm, I think I'm gonna go. You've got some bigger issues to work out, McKenna. Pun intended."

I roll my eyes to the back. "You don't have to leave. That's just stupid crap between me and my stupid sisters."

She nods. "Oh, but I do. I told you, McKenna, I don't do drama. And you're nothin' but."

"Ali, you know you the homie but I'mma bounce too. Y'all really need to try to learn how to get along. Jussayin'," just says Reilly.

I step aside and watch as they head down the stairwell, greeting my mother along the way. My eyes begin to water. I don't understand what is going on with me and why everyone is trying to make like it's my fault, like I'm doing something wrong. I rush into the bathroom and attempt to pull myself together before I have to face my mother and answer the dreaded question that everyone keeps asking me, *What's wrong?* Or worse, *What happened?*

Resolutions

It's a new dawn, it's a new day, it's a new life for me. That's what that old timey singer had to say about whatever was going on in her world. Me and mine? Well I don't know what Nina Simone was thinking. It may be a new year but I've got the same ol' problems and I gotta find a way to escape them. Wish I had her good fortune mojo. My mom loves that song. It's her Sunday morning I'm-about-to-go-in-on-cleaning-my-house ritual and it's playing now, loud and obnoxious from down below, invading my bedroom and my eardrums.

So, though it's maybe too late in the year for it, I've resolved to take a page from Mom's book and make some changes that I can only hope will simplify my crazy existence. Welp, here we go. All I need is to get through the next three years and then I'm free to move on with my life and leave Eden Grove and all it's woes in my rearview mirror. A mirror that's hopefully attached to a better car than Millie's. Wouldn't that just fry her tiny little brain.

So in my resolution for change, here is what I've come up with:

Resolution Numero Uno

Up my weight gain efforts. So far what I've been doing seems to be working – kinda. I mean…well, Nattie and I have only had a couple weigh-ins since making the pact almost two months ago and so far I've gained 5 lbs. Except, my body doesn't really look much different so I'm not too sure where the weight is. I got all excited that one of my most fav tops was slightly too tight suddenly, but upon further investigation I had to face the realization that the development of new boobs had little…well, nothing to do with it.

Resolution Numero Two

Take a break from Simone and Erika. I know right. Strange thing to resolve considering that we've been bestees since like, before time. But it's like, they don't know me. I mean, they know me but they don't understand me. I think well, maybe we *are* growing apart. That's totes possible. I mean, I've heard of it happening with people that have been friends for a very long time. Best Friends Forever overnight becoming Best Friends Never, or worse, Frenemies.

And I feel like one or the other is the path we're on considering Erika actually comes by my house sometimes and just hangs with D'asia. She claims it's just 'cause they share some AP classes and are doing homework, but since when do either of them need help with homework? Seriously. And Simone acts like I don't notice how much time she spends around Karlie Rygluski, which is so obvs her potential gateway to the in-crowd. Soon she'll be officially pointing and laughing at me side by Demitry Haggardy's side.

So maybe apart is where we're headed anyhow. If so, it's better that I accept that now rather than get hurt later.

Resolution Three

Get Gage to finally notice me. Unfortunately, achieving this hinges on the success of Resolution Numero Uno. Hmmm…okay, I'll re-lable this one Resolution Numero Uno point Five. Moving on…

New Resolution Number Three

Have nothing further to do with Millie and D'asia. Those two are perfect for one another and I want no part in their twisted little world. Just because we're sisters doesn't mean we have to deal with one another outside of the requisite familial obligations. From this moment on, I am an only child. No – wait, there's Maddex. Whatev.

"Alijah," my thoughts and note taking are interrupted by my mother's stern voice which means that she's come to give me orders. "Get up. I need you to go with your sisters to Mrs. Sampson's and pick up a few things that she has for me."

"Oh, Mooom," I groan. "Why do I gotta go if Millie and D'asia are already going? How much stuff can it possibly be? Mrs. Sampson is old."

My mother looks confused. "Delilah is 48."

I give her that face that says that I don't get her point.

"Alijah."

I sigh. "Sorry, Mom. It's just that... I mean..."

"What, you three aren't getting along these days. I get it, I'm not dense, Ali. I can slice the tension and serve it for dinner." Mom throws the towel she's been holding over her shoulder before entering my room and taking a seat on my bed. "I don't know what's going on with you girls. Heck, I'm not sure I want to know."

"Well, Mom, if you know something is going on then why are you forcing us to be confined in a car on a road trip together?"

"Because." PAUSE. If I'd said that to her, she would've told me that *Because is not an answer.* Ugh, parents. "Listen, you girls are sisters. Always will be and you've got to learn to work out your differences. So, I'm gonna stay out of it - for now anyway. But I'm not going to work around it, nor will alter my mothering or expectations because of it."

I drop my head. No point in fighting it, I'll never win.

Mom takes my chin in her hand and raises my head so that our eyes meet, then turns it side to side.

"What's going on with you, Squirrel?"

"I don't know what you mean."

Mom sighs, looking me over awkwardly and I shift uncomfortably.

"Fine, you stay here. But you're not off the hook. You won't just lay around this room feeling sorry for yourself all day. You are going to help me with the Sunday house cleaning, which includes laundry and grocery shopping."

I never thought I'd be so happy to be made to do chores. Relief, that should be the Word of the Day.

Mom looks at me awkwardly again, then gently pokes me in the belly. "Besides, you can use a little movement. Have you considered getting back into soccer? I mean, what happened? You used to love that sport? Hm. Well, I'll send your sisters on without you. We'll start with the laundry. Meet me downstairs in five."

So up gets my mom and she heads out my room, strolling along like everything is all good and she just earned Mother of the Year, as I sit with my bottom lip resting on my bedspread wondering, *Did my mother just call me fat?!?*

Laila-"Ali"

What Had Happened Was...

The world is in thaw mode and sooner than later, the ground will be solid and dry and completely visible. The birds will have returned in full force and the only worthy field in town will be ripe for running across with a ball between my feet. For as much as I love winter, I think that I maybe like this time of year just a teeny bit more. And well, not to get ahead of myself, but not too long after, the school year will come to a close, and I gotta be honest – I am sooo looking forward to it.

High school turned out to be such a monumental pain since the whole stupid thing started and it hasn't much improved. Actually, if I'm being real, I'd have to say the opposite has happened and I can sum up my devastation in one particularly deceptive day...

Flashback...

Okay, so it was like thee last day of school before spring break. This particular day is also known as the second greatest day of the school year, which is followed on the list of great days by the last day of school before winter break and preceded by the last day of school before summer break. Got it? Good. Moving on.

I was in high spirits for a change. Okay, so I'll admit I've probs been considerably cranky as of late and admittedly have come to be somewhat of a loner. But I just needed a break from it all and *all* equals: Millie, D'asia, Justin, Reilly, Erika, Simone, and even Nattie. Personally, I think how unselfish of me. I mean, I've given them the freedom to explore Ali-free territory. This allows Erika the opportunity to, in good conscience, "study" with my little sister D'asia. The word study gets airquotes because with all the giggles coming from the room down the hall from me, the two seem to be more social than studious. But my mother is apparently somehow oblivious to all of this. Interesting.

As for Simone, she's taken to spending even more time with her new buds, Karlie Rygluski and Lemethia Duggard. I suspect that it has everything to do with their sophomore status and off-campus lunch privileges that Simone likes to sneak and partake in. She thinks I don't know what's up but, whatev. Truth is, we haven't been the same since she went all #teamhaggardy on me. And whenever those two happen along, it's as though I vanish or possibly have never existed for her in the first place. Again, how awesome am I for backing off? Jussayin'.

And Justin? Well, he was taking to high school just fine so he really didn't seem to have much time for any of us anymore anyhow.

With #teamali seemingly disbanded, it just left Nattie and me but somehow our weight gain-weight loss pact was dividing even us. No secret that Nattie and me had been trading all these habits and ideas from our own experiences in order to help us meet our goals.

Well, something about the camaraderie seemed to amp up Nattie's commitment to her cause. She was eating the salads I brought her from home but soon started including one with school lunch. She'd even gotten to the point of being able to breathe through her sit-ups!

So now Nathalie Flores is eleven pounds lighter and looking good in new jeans that she bought with her birthday money. To her Abuela's dismay and despite her continued objections and insistence that Nattie's gonna like, wither away into nothing, she keeps eating smaller portions and filling the void with whatever fresh, unaltered veggie her mom includes in their evening meal. Good for her [sarcasm].

Believe me, I don't wanna be a hater but how unfair is this? And just what have I gained? Nothing! My skin is kinda jacked most of the time, and I actually got a little winded heading to art class the other day on the top floor at school. And although I picked up another half pound which joyously made my butt slightly bigger as evidenced by the tightening of my jeans around my backside, the struggle with upper body garments kinda offset the accomplishment. So lately I've taken to just wearing sweaters and hoodies and since the only guy that seems to notice my enhanced rear is Tyson Finch, I've also taken to wearing oversized tees to cover it. I suppose I don't want attention *that* bad.

Wait – what was my point? Oh yes, spring time. The morning of the last day of school before spring break I was indeed in high spirits. After a late winter cold snap, we were finally getting the warm weather that we were all too desperate for. So on this day I was awakened early by sunshine rays splaying across my spirit, although not yet across my bedroom. All good. I knew from having watched the news with Laurence the night before that our warm weather trend was continuing and even expected to go up a notch. An unseasonably warm day was just right for an unusually Ali day. So I dug out the large bin labeled *Spring* from beneath the pile of clothes that Mom's been nagging me to put away since forever. I figured my mom would be none too happy about my taking clothes from it prematurely, but chance it 'cause she was being unusually *un*-mom like.

I pull out a faint yellow shirt dress and pair it with black capri leggings and yellow hi-top Cons. I craft the absolute perfect side ponytail, carefully tying a ribbon around my head and twisting it so that the bow dangled in the back [#pinterest #perfectponytails]. Outside of a few recent minor facial blemishes, I feel pretty.

Mom and Maddie's voice can be heard coming from the kitchen below so I brace myself for the it's-too-soon-and-youre-going-to-catch-your-death-of-cold convo before heading down.

"Mo'nin, Awi," says Maddie, looking up from his bowl of cereal.

"Good morning, Maddie," I answer, pausing on the bottom step, and frozen in place under the weight of my mother's questioning gaze. I swear I'm in trouble as I watch her brown eyes move down my partially exposed legs, then up to the yellow ribbon. I'm not sure what to make of the look on her face but her expression softens and she refocuses on the omelet she's making.

"You look nice, sweetie. Very pretty actually," she tells me and I smile and blush.

"Thanks, Mom. Hey...Mom, do you think you can...?" I pause real nervous-like, trying to find the best way to phrase my question.

"What is it, Ali? Can I what?"

"Can you...I mean, do you think it'll be okay if like...well, I'm just saying –"

"No, sweetie, you're not saying anything actually. Just spit it out," she chuckles.

"Concealer," There, I spit it out. "I mean, it's not really make up so I'm wondering if it's okay...if I could wear some...today."

Mom puts her hand on her hip and points her spatula in my direction and I think I remember not breathing for a sec. Make up isn't a thing before you're seventeen, not in our house. It was the rule in Mom's childhood home and it's the same in every Greene Sister household.

"Grab my purse off the couch and come on over here."

I exhale and feel the color drain back into my face, catching my balance before gathering the purse and bringing it to her. She takes it and gestures for me to have a seat on a stool near the island while she finishes her egg and when she's done, she turns her focus to me. She takes a small gold pouch out of the larger bag and starts working on my face.

"So," she begins as she unexpectedly rubs a light pink glittery gloss across my lips, "what's all this about, what's the occasion? Here. Blot. Don't want to be too shiny."

I shrug cause I'm seriously unsure. I just, more than anything, wanted to feel differently than I had been feeling. But I can't tell a mom that. A statement like that opens a whole can of parenting that I really wasn't interested in at the time.

"Nothing special. Just anxious for spring, I guess."

"C'mon, Squirrel. Is it that boy?" Mom's voice gets low and conspiratorial. "What's his name again? Grudge? Gadget?"

"Mom!" I know it's just me, Mom, and Maddie but I just felt horrified. "His name is Gage and no, of course not."

"Is it a new boy?"

"Mom!"

"Don't Mom me. You guys like to try and act as though you're not out here checking out these little boys. I know better than that. You girls can be worse than boys, going all out of your way trying to get them to pay you just the slightest bit of attention."

I say nothing and Mom just looks at me oddly – well, in all due fairness, if her odd look had become a regular thing then she was looking at me quite normally. I try not to give and just offer a gracious smile and thanks for the makeup until she finally releases me.

"Okay. If you say it's nothing, then it's nothing."

"It's nothing."

She watches me for a lingering sec then moves abruptly, putting her tools away and returns to her usual morning habits. I ease from the stool, turning in time to accidentally make eye contact with D'asia. We're both frozen for a sec, like we want to say something but we're waiting for the other to say something first and I was not about to break our mutual vow of silence.

Surprisingly D'asia does speak – sort of. Guess it was more of a mumble that sounded like, "You look pretty."

I think I blushed and almost smiled but I remembered that we don't like each other right now and I could care less what she thinks. I thank her anyhow 'cause my mom would have a spaz attack if I didn't, and walk quickly toward my book bag.

"You're leaving already? No breakfast?" Mom asks.

"I'll eat at school."

"Alijah, don't be silly. Come eat."

"No thanks, I'm not hungry right now. I promise I'll eat when I get to school."

"Are you sure? Everything is ready and you certainly have time."

"I'm sure, Mom. Thanks."

"Oh...okay. But you look so nice in your dress. You shouldn't sit on that dirty bus today. Why don't you ride with your sisters?"

Yeah, nice try, Mom, I think. I glance thoughtlessly at D'asia who averts her eyes and stuffs a piece of toast in her mouth.

"Who should ride with who?" Millie asks as she bounds down the steps, staring at me as though it was my idea; as if I'd want to be confined in a tight space with the likes of her. "Oh, I get it. Ali looks somewhat like a normal human being today so she should get special treatment."

Millie's version of a compliment requires zero acknowledgement. "Don't worry, I have no intention on riding with you."

"Great! I have zero intention on letting you."

"Millie," Mom interrupts. "I would watch that attitude if I were you before you find yourself riding the bus alongside her."

"Oh, c'mon! That's not hardly fair."

"I'll be fine, Mom. I'll take the bus."

"Alijah –"

"It's fine. Totally. Have a good day at work."

"Ha'wa good day, Awi," says Maddex.

I smile at him. "You too, Maddie."

"Ali..." My mom sounds oddly sad when she says my name. I adjust my bag and hurry outdoors.

8 • Lipstick on a Pig

On the surface the day was complete fabs. I was even fooled for a moment and I know better. Has it really been this easy all along? Here I've been doing any and everything I can think of to fatten up and stand out and all it took was a newish yellow dress and lipgloss?

Are you insane?

So. The point of this little journey in time is primarily to illustrate my level of being cursed. Maybe it's a family curse but nah, can't be. I don't know anyone in my family who is doomed to suffer so much pain and torment as I am. For awhile I thought, maaaaybe D'asia would match my suffering to some degree. Y'know, the whole genius/nerd thing. I know, I know, what a terrible sister – no, person – for wishing ill will to my baby sis.

But realistically, a little cursed luck on D'asia wouldn't have been so bad considering she had that genius thing to fall back on. And although that should cause what would feel like a lifetime of torment during her school days, it'll serve her well once those days are behind her. But that isn't how it played out. She got to leave Arthur Ashe a year early, grew boobs over summer vaca, got Millie-style beautiful, and even got a secret boyfriend. Oh! Oh! And to top it off, she nearly got a kiss from Gage Campbell! My – well, it goes without saying. Suddenly, all of the world is just right for the likes of D'asia Raquel McKenna.

Not for me, never for me. I'm not sure at what moment I realized that something was wrong, but at some point, I suspected it. Maybe it was when Mom texted us the Word of the Day: Anathema, meaning a person or thing accursed or consigned to damnation or destruction. Or maybe it was the series of clues that opened my eyes.

Clue Number One: Complimentary Behavior

Oddly, when you're me, this is the most obvious example of a day destined for failure. To the untrained eye it would appear that this was somehow a good day for me, a sign of better things to come. But this type of day isn't without a price.

Clue Number Two: Bubble Guts

Everyone knows that uneasy feeling that you get in the pit of your stomach. You get it when you have to give a speech or you ditched and got caught and some unreasonable teacher is gonna call your mom and straight tattle on you. Well, I had that feeling all day. And not the uneasiness attached to Clue Number One but an actual, physical uneasiness. The type that's hard to describe. Not nervous, not sick. Just not right.

So more about this upset stomach: I make it to the last class of the day before my queasy stomach turns into a kinda painful one. Flashing back to lunch, there wasn't anything out of the ordinary. Since Nattie and me made the weight-pact all that ever really happened was acne and ill-placed fat, so I kinda just went back to my normal eating habits which excluded the previously pretty excessive dose of fried and fatty delish'ness that I'd come to crave throughout the day. Therefore, nothing should've upset the balance.

I glance at the clock, desperate for the bell to ring. And the strangest thing happens and it sorta kinda feels like someone spilled something in my seat except I'm sitting in it so that is not possible. I mean totally, this cannot be going down! I concentrate on being normal and not revealing the panic attack that is happening on my insides while I try and deduce what could be going on with me. All the elements of a real disaster are brewing, including being seated near the middle of the classroom which I attend with Demitry H and Mya F.

I watch the hands of the clock, oblivious to whatever homework is being assigned by Mr. Grayson, occasionally remembering to breathe. I don't fully understand what is happening with me but I do realize that I need to beat the EOD rush while drawing as little attention to myself as realistically possible in the process. But realizing that there is no logical way to make that happen, I opt for plan B – grabbing my bag, springing from my seat, and backing up to the door as casually and quickly as I can, hopeful that somehow no one will notice.

"Alijah?" Mr. Grayson calls.

Well, I had hope. I keep backing up but pretend that I'm doing nothing out of the ordinary. "Yes, sir?"

"Where do you think you're going? I've not yet dismissed anyone."

"I know. I apologize. I have to go...sir."

Mr. Grayson scrunches his face and shakes off the apparent regret at deciding on a career in teaching. "Ms. McKenna, please return to your seat. You will go when everyone else goes."

I'm so sure my face is royally flushed. I struggle to find words as I continue backing to the door, trying my very best to send him a message via my weak telepathy skills but he is so not catching on.

"I apologize on her behalf," Demitry offers. "I dropped a straight pin and, for her, the sound probably rang so loud in her teeny tiny ears...well, she must've thought it was the bell. I promise to be more careful next time."

The class erupts in laughter and I think, for the first time ever,

Demitry Haggardy actually did me a favor. And so, rather than get upset and offer a witty comeback, I use the opportunity to ditch the scene while my teach tries to regain control of his class.

"Oh. My. God," I hear Demitry gasp just before the bell actually rings.

I move as quickly as I can, trying to make it through the hall before it overflows with students, but Demitry is out the class and right on my heels.

"Alijah McKenna, is that *blood* on the back of your pretty dress?"

My suspicions are confirmed and, as if on cue, tears flood the brims of my eyes and I want to keep going and escape this scene by getting to the restroom but the world is a blur and I swear everyone is pointing and laughing, although I can't actually see or process much of anything around me. Before I know it, Demitry and Mya are standing right in front of me.

"Oh McKenna, did you actually wear your best yellow dress during shark week? That wasn't very smart, now was it? As the sister of a little nerd girl like D McKenna, one would think you'd know better. But...well, I guess *she's* the genius, not you."

"Maybe she just got her first period today," Mya correctly suggests.

"No. Way! Oh, this so rich. Can't be! But I mean, it makes perfect sense. She *is* totes underdeveloped. Huh. And you thought you could take my Gagey from me? Please. He wants a woman, not a clueless little girl."

"Yeah, he doesn't want a little girl. Why do you think Demitry's had such a hard time keeping him? Duh, because to him she's like, still a little girl but it's only 'cause we're freshmen of course, but next year–"

"Mya, shut up! O M G!"

"Sorry."

To my dismay I can't form a retaliatory sentence. I'm a wreck and they're all in my face and won't let me by, and worse, I've been at this school for well over seven months and suddenly have no idea where the bathroom is located!

She and Mya take turns saying mean things that I can no longer comprehend. I'm frozen in place and can't figure out what I should be doing. Do I fight back in this condition or get the heck outta dodge? I feel someone grab my arms and I'm relieved to see Erika and D'asia.

"Ali, what's going on? You're crying? Why in the world are you crying?" Erika asks. "And why are you letting Sasquatch pick on you?"

"Sasquatch?" Demitry repeats, sounding appalled.

"Yeah, ya know, Big Foot," she answers, looking down at Demitry's size abnormally large feet. Of course she's insecure about them! They're like a full size too big for her height. Why didn't I think of that?

I want to laugh and give Erika mad props for the burn but I can't get any words out. I knew there were tears in my eyes but I don't think it registered that I was actually crying. I feel 360 degrees of eyeballs on me and simply cannot react.

"Neither of you lame-o's told the imp here how periods work?" Demitry answers for me.

D'asia's eyes become saucers. She pulls me to her and immediately snatches off her sweater and wraps it around my waist. "Oh my gosh, Ali. Of all days, you get your period today?" she asks quietly, respectfully.

"I didn't exactly do it on purpose," I manage to mumble out.

"I know, I know," she says as she ties the sleeves into a knot. "It's just a bad day for a yellow dress. And you two, how dare you? You know, this could easily be you one day."

Demitry scoffs. Like literally scoffs. "Puh-lease. That will never be me. I know better."

"You can leave now," says Erika. "We got it from here. Thank you for absolutely nothing."

After a brief standoff, Demitry announces that she's bored anyway and stalks away with an obedient Mya in tow. Erika screams for the gawkers to find some business before trying to convince me to ignore those stupid girls and telling me in complete motherly fashion how natural my menstrual cycle is. This only serves to further horrify me. And I can't just ignore them, can I? Demitry and Mya just humiliated me in front of kids I have to see every day and I'm s'posed to just let it go?

I feel something hit the back of my head gently just before Demitry's voice rings out, "That's what you need. If you don't know how to use it, I'm sure the nurse can help."

Laughter. More laughter from all around me. Erika and D'asia try to encourage me to go with them. I look down at the small white package resting by my shoe and I stop crying immediately. Just like that, my emotional explosion is no more and I feel completely under control. I stoop down and pick up the tampon, innocent but taunting, despite Erika and D'asia's insistence that I leave it and leave this scene behind.

But what's to lose? I mean, really? This day is going to follow me for the rest of my high school life, and maybe even beyond, and hiding out sooner than later isn't going to change that or lessen the damage. And so I about face, wiping the wetness away and clearing away as many signs of weakness as I can. Demitry's attention is no longer focused on me. She's laughing and saying something to her little clique which now includes Kamahla and, of all people, Gage.

They are laughing and I lose it.

Before I realize that I've even moved, I'm charging down the hall, tampon in one hand, and shortly thereafter, a fist full of Demitry's hair in the other hand. I have no idea of my intention but I know I don't want to fight her. She's yelling for someone to get me off of her, something about me being a crazy person, and without thinking about it, I'm suddenly trying to stuff the tampon into her mouth. Nope, I didn't want to fight her. I just wanted her to shut up!

It isn't clear just how long this scene went on, Demitry flailing and struggling to breathe while I assaulted her with the tampon that she first assaulted me with. Maybe it was 30 minutes or maybe it was 30 seconds, but at some point I'm pulled away I'm assuming by a teacher or some authority figure. Turns out the voice of reason actually belonged to Justin and was enough to calm me.

Justin quickly hurries me from the scene of my crime in time to avoid being caught in the act by "da man" [or in this case it was da woman that I saw shoving students aside while heading in my direction], whilst simultaneously scolding Erika and D'asia for just standing by and watching instead of breaking it up. I glance back, feeling superior as Demitry is helped to her feet. And I gotta admit that it sure made me feel better knowing that the uproar of laughter surrounding me was now directed at her.

But I hadn't expected to feel disturbed when I got a glimpse of *him* standing by looking smug and arrogant. That was when I realized that he was the reason for all this stupid fighting, and there he was just standing by, laughing with his own minions, likely at both me *and* Demitry. He'd been there the whole time, just watching, so totally aware that all of this is ultimately about him and he didn't bother to step in, not for me and not even for his so-called *girlfriend*. And in that moment, surrounded by kids still laughing and joking at my expense and with a teacher mere footsteps away trying to bully just one kid into a confession, it finally hit me. After all the years of trying to get him to pay me just a little bit of attention, in that moment I realized what I should have known all along...what Erika and D'asia tried to warn me about but I wouldn't hear it – Gage Campbell is a jerk!

I yanked free of Justin's grasp and turned back with intention, stopping inches from Gage, fuming and so totes P.O'd! He just keeps laughing thee most irritating, grating laugh I've ever heard and I wonder if he's always been this obnoxious.

"What now?" he asks. "You're such a kid, Ali. Y'know, you can't solve all your problems by fighting. I don't want you so you attack my girl? But what you don't get is that I'm not even into her anymore and I'm def not into you, so why don't you beat it. Don't you need to get home anyway and change your rag?"

He and his friends laugh and high five each other and I, like a person possessed, haul back and –

PAUSE. I don't want anyone to think that I believe that my actions are acceptable and I know I'll at some point regret this for many reasons. And maybe Gage is right, maybe I do use violence as a means to an end at times. But it's too late for quiet reflection. My open palm had already been aimed for his cheek and it would've connected hard had Justin not grabbed me up by the waist and carried me away kicking and screaming about how much of a butthole Gage Campbell really is!

A safe distance away, he returns me to my feet and commences to scolding me. "Ali, what is wrong with you? Why are you being a crazy person?"

"Why do you think we call her Ali-Cat," Erika offers with a chuckle, to which I roll my eyes.

"It isn't funny, Erika. She was going to hit him."

"He deserved it!"

"That isn't the point."

D'asia steps between the two attempting peacemaker status. "Justin, please. We'll take it from here. Now isn't the time for lecturing her."

"Now is not - D, I just pulled her away seconds short of slapping the crap out of Gage Campbell and this is after stopping her from shoving a...a...*a tampon*," [he whispers that word], "down Demitry Haggardy's throat while you two stood by and watched."

"I know, I know. And you're right but I'm asking you, please let it go. For now. Okay?"

"Let it go? Let it go?" The second time he says it, his voice rises like three octaves.

Erika and D'asia nod. "Let it go."

"Yeah, well, you know who's not going to let it go? *Your mother!*" Justin throws his arms in the air and walks away in a huff. "You girls...just...crazy..."

D'asia turns to face me. "He's right. Mom's gonna be so ticked when she finds out."

I shrug it off and try not to care.

"Ali, c'mon, let's get you out of here. I'm certain someone is looking to turn you in. You don't want to ruin spring break for yourself. Maybe we can hold off the wrath until after." Erika takes my arm but I snatch away.

I shake my head. "Whatever. Just go."

"Ali," D'asia says in a soft tone. "This is your first period. Just let us help get you set right."

My feelings about my *little* sister offering to help me through my first period was totes horrified. "No."

"We're just trying to help."

"Well I don't want your help. I just want to be left alone."

I snatch my bag that Erika's been holding for me and retreat to the bathroom and rush to the furthest stall, lock the door, and let all my emotion about the events of the day pour out as quietly as possible.

Amends

The ride home is silent which is crazy surprising and kinda scary considering, but can't say I wasn't relieved. Erika was right, some authoritarian who opted not to intervene on the front end, ratted us out after the fact. I was so sure that Mom was going to lay into me the entire way for having been required to pick me up from the Principal's office, but she said nothing.

So there we were, all crammed into that tiny little office listening to Demitry, as expected, blame everything on me. And

I'm sorry, I was just in no mood to discuss any of it, and so I refused to defend myself or offer any sort of generic explanation and was therefore the decided perpetrator. The honor of this title earned me a one week suspension while the Haggardy kid got off with a warning.

As it turned out, D'asia had already filled our mother in on the ugly truth of what'd gone down. But because my mom wasn't a witness and I refused to talk, they say I gave no other choice but to have them decide in Demitry's favor. So sure it had nothing to do with her status as the Superintendent's kid [insert sarcastic eye roll here]. I didn't care. After what she did, being suspended was a kindness. The longer they banned me from that place, the better.

I climbed out of the car wearing the jeans and gray long sleeve top that Mom brought for me to change into, and hurried into the house. I caught eye contact with D'asia who was standing partway down the staircase. I'm totes unclear how I feel about her opening her big mouth to Mom. Wasn't sure if she was trying to help me out or get me in trouble.

"I'm going to take a shower," I offered softly when I heard Mom come through the door.

"Oh, she speaks," Mom's tone is dripping sarcasm. "Where was your voice when we were in your Principal's office and you were taking the rap for all this?"

"You took the blame, Ali?" D'asia says as she runs down the steps and comes toward us. "Why would you do that?"

"D'asia, stay out of this...please." I don't want to fight with my mother and sister or, for that matter, talk about any of this. I only wanted to shower but it quickly became pretty apparent that they weren't going to let it go as easily as I had. "Guys, I had a fight at school. I hit Demitry and –"

"The way I heard it you more like tried to make her eat a tampon," Mom interrupts. I can only stare at her, not sure if I should go on. "I mean if you gone tell it, tell it."

Mom and I stare at each other and I completely forget what I was gonna say. Then the strangest thing happened. My mother starts laughing, I mean really laughing. She's bent at the waist and when she stands upright I see tears in her eyes.

I'm crazy startled and don't know how to react. All I can do is look to D'asia who's looking at me with just as much confusion. I look back to my mother who is trying to speak but she's laughing way too hard...so I start to laugh. And before I know it, D'asia's laughing like crazy too!

The three of us are in complete hysterics when we hear the front door open and see Millie come in. We stop laughing, trying our best to compose ourselves despite our eyes being all puffy and red and wet.

Millie paused and gave us a look somewhere between confusion and disgust. There was a Word of the Day for it once: Incredible... incredilust...incredu-something but there is another, bigger word for it. Look it up. "What are you three baffooning about? I heard you got into some fight today. Shouldn't you be on time-out or something?"

And like that, laughter erupted once again. For no reason. For every reason. And it just felt good. Millie shakes her head at us and stalks away, probably upset because she assumes we're laughing at her, and that thought just made me laugh harder.

"Okay, okay," Mom opened, trying hard to force herself to calm down. "Let's be serious. C'mon, girls, I'm trying to be serious here. I have to be motherly now. Ali, talk to me. Tell me what's been going on. What was today about?"

"I mean, D'asia told you right? I got my period and those dumb girls –"

"No, I don't mean that. I mean the whole of today."

I sigh and flick the laugh tears that are mingling with the unexpected sad tears from beneath my eyes. I told my mom everything. How it sucks to be me, middle child and sister of a beauty queen who hates me and genuis-slash-beauty queen on the rise. How I'm always forced to take a back seat to them. How hard it is to be so small in a family of such bodacious women. I confess the pact with Nattie and how I hoped that it would solve my problems by helping me grow curves like everyone else.

"That explains the skin issues and weight gain," Mom says as she caresses my chin.

I avert my eyes, ashamed and embarrassed.

Mom sighs. "Squirrel, you're beautiful."

"You're supposed to say that."

She nods, conceding. "Yeah, I suppose I am. That doesn't make it any less truthful. You *are* beautiful. No different than Millie. No different than D'asia. You're only built different than us, and that's okay. Own it. Love it. You think we don't know how you feel?"

"I know you don't. Look at you, Mom. All of you. All the women around me are brickhouses."

My mother chuckled and shook her head. "Sho' ya right about that."

"Great Mom, that helps."

She laughed and put her arm around my shoulder. "Look, you're right. But you don't think Millicent has insecurities? She may never admit it but c'mon. Have you seen those stick legs and knobby knees? And me? I blossomed much later than my sisters and they teased me relentlessly. But my time came and yours will to – in it's own time. Don't rush it and don't force it or you may get it the way you *don't* want it. And besides, I like how you're made... just like my mother was."

Mom's eyes soften and get shiny. I grab her hand and squeeze it softly.

"Hey, Ali, I'm sorry," said D'asia.

"For what?"

She shrugs and averts her eyes before looking back to me. "I dunno, everything. For what I said to you, for being mean. But mostly for not being a good sister. I know...more than anyone else, I know. I got caught up, I guess. People are finally paying attention. I was noticed for something other than what random fact I knew or what grade I got on a paper. And for the first time I didn't feel like this weirdo freak just 'cause I can retain more info than many others."

"Most," I chuckle.

"Okay, most. I understand how you feel but I think...I think I just wanted to pretend that I've always been accepted. Forget that I was ever overlooked and teased."

I smile at my little sister. "Eh, it's all good. I s'pose I was the occasional culprit. Count it as a little payback. Now we're even."

"Awww, my girls," Mom whines, wrapping her arms around the both of us. "This...this is what I like to see."

D'asia and I just laughed and shook our heads.

Grad Student

I'm still trippin' about what happened that day. My brain is still like, how? How did I miss that?"

"Duh, I'm so sure it's cuz you were off *pretending* to be a second year," Erika answers Simone without looking up from the Ransom Riggs book she's reading.

"Don't hate." Simone leans over my new dresser so that she can get a close-up view of herself in the mirror. She dabs a super glossy pink on her lips, one with so much shimmer that it looks more like she's wearing lipstick than teen-friendly gloss.

Erika looks up from her book and joins me in watching Simone contort her face into all different expressions. First she puckers and sucks her cheeks in tight before smiling super broad showing off like, every tooth in her mouth. She's feeling super extra since her mom just brought her back from Ms. Coretta's shop getting her hair done, a weave that hangs all the way down to the middle of her back.

I swallow my tiny bit of jealousy. Mom is not going for my getting a weave, says my hair is long enough. I say, what girl's hair is ever long enough? I mean, seriously? Old folks are always saying how they remember what it is to be our age and then they say crap like that.

Simone starts to twist and turn, alternating poses and flipping her hair around for some imaginary photographer that only she can see. Erika stands and walks over and grabs Simone by the waist, guiding her away from the vanity – or from *her* vanity.

"Okay, that's enough, Queen Bee. Focus on us now."

"Oh my goodness. How focused are you while reading a book?"

"We all know I'm capable of multitasking. You on the other hand..."

"Yeah, shoulda told you before now but peeps don't generally read books while they're hanging out. But if you can do that, I can do this."

Simone rushes back to the mirror again and flips her hair back and around a couple more times before Erika grabs her and guides her back to my bed.

"Stay."

"I'm so not Bette Middleton, thank you. Anywayz, you gotta admit, this hair is the most, right? At first, my mom was not going but then my dad comes in all, *it's my baby girls birthday and I'm gonna one up you and get her a spa day*. So for this week's hair appointment, Mom decides to go hard as a belated gift. Cool, right? It's Peruvian."

I don't know my weaves and therefore this revelation of my friend's hair ethnicity is confusing to me. But being that I don't want to look silly, I nod and smile and let her continue. "Divorce is incredible. All those kids crying and complaining because their parents are breaking up are just totes redic. They should be rejoicing. I swear it's like thee best gift your parents can ever give to you."

"What? What kinda nonsense is that?" Erika asks, clearly annoyed. "You're not even making sense right now."

"It makes total since. You think it's harsh because you don't know any better. Unfortunately for you, your parents are all *we're still in love and wanna be together*. That's unfortunate. I'm telling you, divorce is like, major. Your mom's trying to outdo your dad, your dad trying to outdo your mom. Your new stepparents are trying to win your approval. Buying affection is a complete win-win."

"That's sick."

"You're insane," I say, falling backwards on my bed.

"I'm right is what I am," Simone states.

My life is pretty much back to normal, whatever that means. Mom grounded me for half of my break. I dunno, it was a kinda confusing sitch. She beamed all sorts of proud for how I stood up to Demitry Haggardy but then said that she had to punish me because she can't let me think that fighting is an acceptable form of conflict resolution. Also, there's the blurred line of whether or not I actually fought Demitry as much as I tried to suffocate her. Guess when you look at it that way, some discipline is in order.

But considering that the school had already issued a punishment called suspension and facing everyone that witnessed the debacle upon my return being a punishment in and of itself, she figured she'd give me the opportunity to enjoy some parts of my school vaca.

"Anyways, what were we talking about before my parents divorce? Oh, yeah, Ali-Cat's brutal showdown! I'm still so bummed that I wasn't there that day," says Simone. "Probably best I wasn't. I'd have totally kicked her butt for you."

Erika makes the *psht* sound and Simone is all taken aback and wondering why she did it.

"You would've risked breaking a nail?"

"Under the right circumstances, yes." Erika and Simone stare each other down for a few seconds. "Eh, you're probably right. I don't play messing my hair up. Oh! Guess who wants your number?"

"Me?" I ask, so shook.

"Yeah you, weirdo."

I groan involuntarily. The strangest thing happened as a side effect of my altercation. When I finally returned to school, I wasn't teased the way that I thought I'd be. I mean, of course I was teased but not like I thought I'd be. Mostly kids were giving me props for standing up for myself.

The other odd thing that happened as a result of standing up to the mean girl who pointed out that I'd started my period to every student within earshot, was that all these guys were starting to take notice of me. Sure, it was all I wanted before but under these circumstances, it's kinda awkward. Not to mention all the guys that want to know me better are the ones I'd never want to know. Actually, I was only trying to get one boy to notice and boy do I regret that now.

"You're groaning? You're kidding me." Simone grabs a pillow and throws it at me. I catch it in front of my face. "You went in on some stupid get fat pact so boys would look at you and now they are and you groan?"

"That's not why...well, not exactly why I...I mean...anyway, who?"

"Who what?" Simone's attention has moved on to her cell and the selfie's she's posing for.

"Who, Monie? Who wants my number?" I throw the pillow back at her being certain to hit her in the head and mess with her perfect 'do.

"Hey!" she squeals, jumping from the bed and stomping to the mirror to adjust her Peruvian hair. "Christian."

I scrunch my face, thinking hard and trying to figure out who she could be talking about. I look to Erika who looks as dumbfounded as I feel.

"Who is Christian?" I ask but she's too busy posing like the paparazzi is hanging incognito in my bedroom. "Simone."

"What?"

I get up and grab my robe from the back of my door and carry it to the mirror, stepping in front of her and carefully hanging it over.

"Hey!" she cries out.

"Seriously, Simone? You look the same way you looked like four minutes ago. Now, Christian? Elaborate?"

"Magnusson?" Erika asks. "You are *not* talking about Mag, are you?"

"Yeah, Mag," Simone answers casually, like it's no big deal. She pulls out a piece of gum and pops it in her mouth and then skips across my room to my desk and flips open my laptop.

Erika and I look at one another in awe before Erika speaks.

"Mag is a junior and like, stupid popular. Why would he possibly want Ali's number?"

"Hey," I cry out.

Erika shrugs. "Sorry."

"I dunno, something about he loves petite girls and hates Demitry. He's friends with Karlie...told her he thinks you're cute."

Mag thinks I'm cute? Ohmagosh, I'm like dying on the inside because Mag thinks that *I* am cute! Me! Okay, so Mag [who's name I just learned is actually Christian – totes adorb!] is a total hottie and star of the boys baseball team. Every girl knows who he is and knows he only dates upperclasswomen, so no way a freshie has a shot! He's so hot, even cuter than Gage what's-his-face used to be. Same color as me with the bushiest eyebrows, full pink lips, and the biggest, deepest dimples I've ever seen. He's even got his ear pierced and I hear he has a tattoo on his right shoulder but Idk if that's just a rumor some girls started just to make him sound that much hotter.

I'm in the middle of mentally picking out my wedding dress and venue for my future marriage to "Mag" Magnusson when a loud thud startles me back to reality. My gorge new kids, Maggie and Mag Jr, are replaced with Simone and Erika and my evil mother-in-law is now Millie standing in my doorway, looking agitated with her hand on her hip and a large box on the floor in front of her.

"Drama much?" I inquire.

"Lame much?" she retaliates. "I think, yes."

"What do you want?"

She points to the box. "Uhm, you think you wanna come and help set up this stupid graduation party? It *is* for you?"

"Please tell me that box isn't full of tampons," Simone says as she creeps over and peaks inside. "Hashtag gross, guys. This family is so weird."

"How does that make sense, Millie? Why would I set up my own graduation party? You and D'asia didn't have to do that."

"Uhm, how 'bout 'cause D'asia and me did the family the courtesy of getting our period at a normal age."

"You're kidding me."

"Not hardly."

"Not fair. Mom!"

"Mom, tell Ali that she needs to help!"

"Millie," Mom calls from some place in the distance. "Ali's the Graduate, she does not have to help."

I win and do a victory lap of sticking my tongue out at my sister. She rolls her eyes and picks up the box.

"I'd throw a tampon at you but I'm scared you might try to suffocate me with it."

I pause, unsure how to respond. But Millie's expression is actually one of a normal person and she even smiles at me before turning to head downstairs to decorate. I smile in response. Now I'm certain that Millie had something to do with the fact that Demitry and her little clique haven't given me any grief since my return to school. I knew for sure that there was no way that Demitry would let me live it down, but instead would keep my devastation going as long as possible. But to my utter surprise, Demitry, Mya, and Kamahla didn't say anything to me when I got back and haven't since.

"Alijah!" Erika and Simone scream simultaneously, signifying that they've been calling my name repeatedly.

"Huh?"

They just shake their heads at me and we all collapse in laughter.

Redrum

I sit in the corner of the couch with my feet tucked beneath me, eating the Neapolitan butter cream cake that Aunt Vee created especially for me based on a recipe that I found on Pinterest. It's what I imagine heaven to taste like. I've been quasi-fantisizing about my future wedding with Mag while observing the room filled with family and friends. Makes me feel so happy seeing everyone getting along, even Nattie and Erika. Surprise, surprise! My take on this pigs fly moment is that Erika's unexpected friendship with D'asia helped her to realize that we *can* have friends outside of our little childhood clique [although she refuses to make the same concession for Reilly who's chatting up my little cousin Taleya instead].

I wouldn't dare share my inner revelation with my mom but I'm kinda realizing that while I was being all down and life sucks, although no doubt justified, I discounted the value of one thing - a family's love. Sure, they all tease me and give me loads of grief, but they're here for me, celebrating my crossover into womanhood same as they did for Millie and D'asia and every cousin that preceded me.

They came without hesitation bearing gifts, cash, food, and unfortunately [not really] totes embarrassing stories about me as a kid, which is kinda like the secondary point of this type of event - the roast. Some I've heard a million times and others are surprising and new.

"Chile, lemme tell you sumthin' else 'bout little miss Alijah Dominique! My girl don't play. Uh uhn, my baby girl go hard with everything she do," Aunt Vee says, like, super prideful.

"Everything but academics," says Auntie Nay, which is like so unnecessary of her. But what can I say? Always gotta be one hater at the party.

"Nah, there you go. The girl do just fine. She pass her grades, don't she? Everybody can't be as academically inclined as you want them to be. She smart. She learn better by doing than by readin' them books, is all. And if memory serve, you was a bit more idiot than savant when you was her age."

Auntie Nay's face turns beet red when Tee Tee Yashi laughs and high fives her big sister. I stuff a slightly too large piece of cake in my mouth to keep myself from literally LOL'ing. This is why I love my Auntie Vee, she always tells it like it is. Everyone in the room laughs freely but for some reason I peep that I'm the one getting the stink eye. I hold my breath for I feel this will somehow suppress an eye roll. Idky but I think this and only this tactic works.

"Whatever, Vee. You know I'm just trying to look out for my niece."

"Girl, Nija ain't cranking out the high marks in every subject either," Mom chimes in, to my surprise. I mean, it's not like I don't think my family thinks highly of me but I'm used to being the brunt of everyone's joke. They mean no harm but it's like when my dad died – the belief that Ali doesn't need comforting because she's tough and she can handle it. It's nice to be recognized as a normal teenage girl for a change.

Cousin Nija, who so clearly is the most disinterested in being here considering that she's spent all evening in the corner of the room texting, FB'in, and snapchatting, looks up, surprised to hear her name. She is not as tough as me and I think I see her feelings hurting. I laugh. Sorry, I can't stand her.

"Hey!" she whines in her bratty voice.

"Sorry, niecey, but your momma came at my baby girl first. You just got caught in the crossfire."

"Now, Dette, you know you are not right," Nay says.

"Nay, please. You know I am."

My mom standing up for me feels good. I sit my plate down and cross over to where she's sitting and throw my arms around her neck, whispering, "Thanks, Mom."

"You're welcome, *Ali-Cat*."

"Ohmahgaaahd," says Nija, clearly annoyed. "I didn't even do anything and y'all just picking on me out the blue. Momma, can we go, please?"

My second surprise of the day comes when Millie stalks over to where Nija has been hiding out. "Oh shet up and quit being such a brat. And get off your phone and participate with your family, geez." Millie snatches the phone and holds it out of reach.

Nija squeals and reaches for her phone but Millie keeps moving it just out of her grasp. "Millie, quit playing!"

Auntie Nay looks to my mother who shakes her head and laughs. "Millicent, give the girl her phone back before she loses her mind. God forbid she miss a moment of telling the world how she feels and how embarrassing we all are."

Millie drops the phone beside Nija, who snatches it up and immediately sticks her nose in the screen.

"Ugh, y'all just be the most," she complains. "I don't even know why you trying to be all on Ali team anyway, Millie. You don't even like her."

"I don't *have* to like her, I *love* my sister, what are you talking about? Just because we don't get along in a way that the world understands, doesn't mean that I don't like her. I will burn this world down for Ali and D'asia, don't you forget it."

"Please," Nija scoffs. "I heard what went down at Wilma Rudolph with Demitry. You know this town is small. You wasn't snatching nothin' and nobody up for Ali then, was you?"

Millie looks taken aback and I unconsciously lean in a bit closer, curious as to what she has to say. In the time that's passed since the big fight, Millie hasn't said anything to me directly about it. I'm not so sure that Nija isn't right.

"No, I wasn't because I wasn't there. But I assure you Demitry hasn't and will not say one more thing out of place to Ali for the rest of their days at Wilma Rudolph."

"I knew it," I yell involuntarily. "After what went down, she totes had the upper hand and she won't even look me in the eye now."

"She better not either. Look, I respect the Social Status Code set forth by all the A-listers before me, and Demitry def earned her spot amongst this elite group from her early days at Arthur Ashe. And I can't fight your battles and protect you and D'asia from all the dysfunction and cruelty of the It Cliques and In Crowds of the world. There are haves and have-nots and that's just the way it is, has been, and always will be. But I'm three years older. If I used my status to protect you girls from the harsh realities of life, what good would it do you when I'm gone? But, she crossed the line and forgot her place and must be put on time out. If she ever hopes to earn *my* crown, she will behave. This may be my final year at Wilma Rudolph but my wrath is far-reaching and she knows it."

The room falls silent. I mean, beyond the Queen B [how fitting] playing in the background, it's like dead silent. I've never heard Millie break it down like this and I'm pretty sure no one else has either and no one knows what to say. She's like an It-girl politician. So instead of finding these elusive words, I look to D'asia who picks up my message and we jump up and run to Millie, wrapping our arms around her and laugh at how uncomfortable we know we're making her.

"Touching," Nija says sarcastically and returns her focus to social media.

"Aww, Millie, you don't totally suck after all," Simone blurts out thoughtlessly.

"Okay, okay," Millie squirms and pushes gently until she's out of our grasp. We let her go but smile as we watch her take a seat next to Mom.

"Ohhh, I'm so proud of you," says our mom, pulling Millie into her bosom, also taking pleasure in her discomfort.

"Gosh, Mom! I wouldn't've said anything had I known you guys would get all weird."

Mom finally frees Millie, who quickly moves across the room and sits beside Aunt Vee – who wraps an arm around her and pulls her close but Millie doesn't object.

"Okay, so moving on to another but slightly less emotional subject," Auntie Donna opens, "Jackie told me about the Valentino's Laurence bought you! How did I miss this purchase?"

"He did. Got them for our anniversary."

PAUSE. Valentino's. You recall. The ones that I wore to school when I was trying to get stupid Gage Campbell's attention and I broke the heel and then me and Millie and D'asia tried to fix it with Gorilla Glue. Valentino's. My heart stops and judging from the look on my sister's faces, theirs does too.

"How in the world? If they're the ones that I'm thinking of, aren't they like, $800?"

I repeatedly swallow the throw up that keeps being in my mouth. *Stay cool, Ali. She doesn't suspect a thing.*

"Yes, girl. He assured me that he didn't pay full price though. It's a long story but he was able to get them for a third of the retail price. But when they're on my feet, they look like every dollar that they actually cost!"

The auntie's laugh but my head is swooning. I mouth the words *eight hundred dollars* to Millie who shakes her head in disappointment. Guess that's another nice thing Millie did for me. Didn't make me feel worse about wearing and destroying Mom's shoes by telling me their actual dollar value. But now, I just feel like such a jerk.

"Well, go get 'em. I have got to see these up close. You know I would give my left pinky toe for them pink Rockstuds."

"Ooh, yes, put them on," says Mrs. Kirkwood, Simone's mom and I just want to smash her face with a couch cushion for like three long minutes.

Mom, ever anxious to show off new goods, jumps up all smiles and gloating. She rushes off in the direction of her bedroom and as though we have but one mind between us, Millie, D'asia, Erika, Simone, and me all jump from our seats at the same time mumbling incoherent and unidentifiable excuses for why we need to leave the house at once. Sure, everyone else in the room is thoroughly confused but that isn't our concern. We are nearly out the door and safely to sweet freedom when we hear –

"ALIJAH DOMINIQUE McKENNA!!!!!!!!!"

Well, life was fun while it lasted. But judging from the several octave increase in Mom's voice, I assume that the glue we used didn't hold as well as we hoped it would. And with that said, I gotta go, so I guess that kinda makes this like, quite literally...The End!!

Acknowledgements

Every girl needs a superhero…particularly little brown girls. Okay, so Ali may not be that but I wanted my little brown nieces to have a female voice in this vast fictitious world that they could identify with – but also that all young girls could identify with. Though I started this project at the behest of The Little Jakes Girl [who thought it unreasonable that I had all these books that she was not allowed to read], I've since amassed a small collection of young girls who I love and to whom I dedicate this.

Kyla Simone, Ameena Simone, Erika, Bella, Gabby, Angel, Amaya, Faith, D'azhane, Monica, Vicky, and baby Victoria, and all the other unnamed girls who are just as special, know that you are beautiful. Whether you are dark, light, medium [or sans] brown, tall or small – YOU are beautiful and perfect just as you are.

My words of wisdom to you are in the name of the title font - "Girls are Weird. And that's okay."

Love you all!
Tia

Miki Starr has authored mainstream, urban, literary, and science fiction, mystery, erotica, and poetry.

This is her foray into the world of young-adult fiction.

She is a wife and loving mother of one.

Originally from Chicago, Illinois, she now lives just outside of Minneapolis, MN where she works in graphic and web design.

www.mikistarr.com/books

www.ingramcontent.com/pod-product-compliance
Lightning Source LLC
Chambersburg PA
CBHW022200170626
46807CB00005B/2292